TH

LAST LAUGH

MICHELLE DOREY

The Hauntings Of Kingston
6

DEDICATION

To the real life Sharon, Peter, Spenser and Hannah. That was some tale you shared!

To the lovely village of Westport, Ontario

And as always, to Jim. Who ever thought getting old would be so much fun, huh?

CONTENTS

ACKNOWLEDGMENTS

I am indebted to the kind assistance of the librarians at The Westport Library, Brockville Library, Queen's University Library. Their interest in this tale and enthusiasm for this story were a tremendous help in bringing this tale to life.

ONE

This is by far the easiest move I've ever made." Sharon wiped a smudge from the cabinet door before easing it shut. She glanced over at her husband, Peter, when he flopped down onto the kitchen chair. Even though he feigned being overwhelmed by work, the twitch of his lips gave him away.

"Easy for you!" Peter reached for her, pulling her close. "*You* only organized the kitchen. However *I* did three rooms upstairs *and* the sunroom."

"You're so hard done by, aren't you? You lugged the wicker furniture in and made the beds. Admit it. You had the easier job." Smiling, she gave his hair a little tug.

"Hey!" He took her hand and held it. "One thing I will admit is that this move was one of the cheapest I've ever done. There was barely anything to move. I still can't get over the fact that they included all the furniture in the sale."

"And so many antiques! It was definitely the clincher when we first looked at the house." With a sweep of her hand, she continued. "Everything fits perfectly in a century home like this. Anyone looking for a Bread and Breakfast with country charm will be totally smoked."

She eased away and stepped over to the counter. As she filled the kettle with water she peered out at the fireflies sparking in the early evening. It was reminiscent of her childhood, playing outside with her sisters, trying to catch their magic in a mason jar.

Peter's voice brought her back to the present, "I'm not sure how things will work for Hannah when we have paying guests. She's already claimed that bedroom in the newer addition to the house. I wish she'd taken the pink bedroom next to us. But having her very own bathroom sealed the deal, I guess." He stifled a yawn, folding his hands over his stomach.

"It'll work out. I remember being nineteen and wanting more of my own space. Plus, she'll only be here for the odd weekend. I just wish she could have found work in the village. It will be hard not having her around all the time." Sharon's smile faded as she set the teapot on the counter and plopped two bags into it. Her baby girl had grown up too fast. Already, their oldest child, Spencer, had established his life half-way across the world, teaching school. Now Hannah was leaving the nest, working in the city.

As if on cue, Hannah entered the kitchen and took a seat next to her father. "My room's all done."

Sharon caught the wink her daughter threw at her father before the teen quipped, "It's even up to Mom's white-glove standard—dusted, vacuumed and you could bounce a quarter off the bed."

"Forgive me for wanting to live in an orderly, clean home!" She smiled at Hannah, "Want some tea? I'm making chamomile. It might help us sleep better considering it's our first night here."

"Sure. And if there's any butter tarts left, I'll take one—that is, if Dad hasn't snarfed them all."

The teasing affection in Hannah's eyes when she smirked at her father touched Sharon's heart. Waiting for the kettle and gazing around the large, revamped country kitchen replete with stainless appliances and granite counters, there was a warmth in her chest. This was everything she'd ever dreamed about —

a gorgeous home in a quaint village setting. The bonus was she'd be her own boss, running a business.

The stress of social work, commuting hundreds of miles between rural schools, had taken its toll over the years. It was better to live a simpler life in a picturesque village. And nestled between Foley's Mountain and two lakes, the scenery was a natural draw for tourists.

She filled the teapot with steaming water and then grabbed the package of butter tarts from the fridge. Peter helped get plates and mugs from the cabinet before setting the table for their evening snack. He even placed her favourite yellow napkins neatly beside each of the plates.

"How's that?" There was a playful glint in his eye. "I folded them diagonally, with the corner facing out."

Sharon rolled her eyes at him. She wasn't that bad, was she? Yeah, she was. The little things Peter did showed how much he cared for her happiness. "Excellent job." She poured the tea.

The blare of voices exploded from the hall!

Sharon jerked, almost scalding herself with hot tea. What the hell? The TV in the family room had blasted on, becoming louder by the second. A quick look at Peter showed that he was as confused as she was.

"Something must have fallen onto the remote. I'll go check." He stood up.

Hannah glanced over at her mother, "Dad's probably right. There are still books and pictures piled up on the coffee table. I meant to put them away, but I ran out of steam." She reached for a tart and bit into it.

Abrupt silence followed before Peter came back into the kitchen, shrugging his shoulders. "The monitor must have picked up on the podcast I was listening to on my laptop. I was positive I paused it, but just to be on the safe side, I shut everything down."

Sharon nodded. "I'll check the TV and laptop before we go to bed. I've got a full day tomorrow and the last thing I need is that monitor blasting Joe Rogan in the middle of the night." Peter was a whiz with numbers and could assess a spreadsheet of financials with a mere glance. But aside from his photography hobby, with anything tech-oriented, he was... well, challenged.

Hannah finished her tea and got up to set her things in the dishwasher. "I'm going up now. I've got a ton of emails and texts to answer before I go to sleep." She paused, putting her hand on her father's shoulder, "I'll help you with the hot tub tomorrow. It would be great if it was up and running before I have to leave." Her eyebrows pulled together when she looked at Sharon, "What's on tomorrow's agenda for you? Anything I can do to help?"

Sharon couldn't help the swell of pride in her chest gazing at Hannah. Her daughter was always ready to lend a hand without complaint. Not only that, but she was radiant with startling blue eyes and full lips that were usually turned up in a warm smile. Kind and attractive; her daughter had an impressive combination.

"I'm organizing my office and then I'd like to get a start on my website. I appreciate the offer, but I really need to get up to speed with doing more on-line work."

Oh, to grow up in the age of the internet, like Hannah. Working on-line, creating platforms was something the girl could do as easily as breathe. What was intuitive to Hannah required Sharon reading a litany of instructions while trying not to scream with frustration. But she had to learn this and get good at it. Hannah wouldn't always be there to hold her hand. If she really wanted to get her B&B up and running, she had to have an online presence.

"Okay. I'm sure you'll nail this, Mom." She leaned down to plant a kiss on Sharon's forehead before saying 'good night'.

"She's right. You're better at this stuff than you give yourself credit for." Peter reached across the table and squeezed her hand, "But if you get really stuck, I'll lend you some of my expertise." His eyebrows bobbed before he chuckled. "At a price."

She shook her head. Men. "I can't afford you, Mr. C.F.O. Besides which, I want it done right." Smirking, she rose to clear the table.

He took the mug from her hand, "I'll get this. You check on the TV and my laptop. I'll be upstairs waiting for you to have your way with me."

"You wish." She grinned, contradicting the exaggerated eye roll. His crazy sense of humor had been another thing she'd been attracted to when they'd met... OMG, almost twenty-five years ago! Where did the time go?

She paused in the doorway leading to the living and dining room. All was quiet in there, only the grandfather clock in the corner ticked steadily. Illumination from the streetlight shone through the gigantic picture window highlighting the leather sofa and oversized oak coffee table. This was a room they would use when they had guest bookings. The home was ideal for a B&B with a self-sufficient annex that could be closed off, giving everyone privacy.

Wandering down the hall, past the small, two-piece bath, she entered the family room. The flickering of the overhead light caught her attention, and she paused for a moment, staring up at it. The bulb was probably due to be changed soon; the usual problem with incandescent lights. She'd replace it with an LED.

On the low sea-chest that served as a coffee table, Peter's laptop lay sandwiched between a stack of books on one side and a tower of DVD's on the other. Even though they usually streamed movies on-line, the old favorites were hard to part with.

She opened the laptop. Yep; Peter had set his computer to sleep, not shut down. With an amused shake of her head she clicked the mouse pad, waiting for it to shut down. Yawning, she got up to check the TV monitor. The screen was entirely black, not even the small light in the lower right corner was lit.

She bent to examine the power bar resting on the floor. What the hell? The plug for the monitor wasn't even connected. Yet it had blared on, not even ten minutes before. Her forehead tightened as she stared at the power bar. Hannah must have beat her to it, stopping there before going upstairs for the night. That had to be it.

She glanced around the room, inspecting dim corners before she doubled checked that the door to the sunroom and the outside were locked. She was probably being paranoid, a left-over from city-life, but it didn't hurt to be careful. It was their first night in their new home, their first night in the tiny village.

When she turned to go back through the house to the main set of stairs, the hair on the back of her neck tingled. A gossamer brush against her cheek made her stop short. The feeling was faint, like walking through a cobweb, but it was definitely there and then gone.

Her heart leapt into her throat as she stood rooted to the spot. It felt like something was in the room with her, watching. Oh God. The eerie feeling brought back a memory from long-ago days. It came rushing back to her as she hurried from the room. She'd been only a child, eight-years-old, seeing her grandmother smiling down at her as she lay in her bed, only to learn the next morning that her Nan had passed during the night.

The same sensation of wonder and fear from that night long ago shot up her spine. Sharon gripped the banister as she walked up the stairs, trying to make sense of it. Was it the house, so similar to the one where she'd grown up? That had to be it. As for that faint feeling on her cheek... maybe it was fatigue. Settling into an unknown place was bound to put one on edge, even if this was her dream home.

She took a deep breath. Yes. Probably one of those things, or maybe even a faint breeze from the window had brushed her skin.

When she entered their bedroom, there was a definite sense of relief seeing Peter propped up in bed, reading his tablet. She let out a soft sigh, walking past the king-sized bed to enter their bathroom to brush her teeth and get ready for bed.

As she shrugged into her robe, she pushed the memory of her childhood aside. It had been a strange phase of her life that ended when she entered junior high. She was an adult now, slightly stressed from all the changes in her life—a new house and a new career. Who wouldn't feel the strain? Her imagination getting the best of her was perfectly reasonable.

Right?

As she got into bed, she made a mental note to check with Hannah in the morning. The eerie feeling might not be real, but that the monitor had been unplugged niggled in the back of her mind. It had to have been Hannah who'd done that. Duh. What else could it possibly be?

TWO

The next morning, the first rays of the September sun flowed like golden honey through the window into their bedroom. Sharon eased out of the nest of sheets, taking care not to wake Peter. The snuffled snores coming from the bundled blankets next to her assured her *that* was unlikely.

She dismissed thoughts of the night before as she looked around the spacious bedroom. Even without that first jolt of coffee, the excitement of being in their new home buzzed through her as she made her way to the adjoining bathroom.

There was so much to do to settle in and make the house their own. As she went about her morning ritual, she made a mental list of the things she wanted to accomplish that day. First, a batch of blueberry muffins, Hannah's favorites—then onto emptying the box of framed family photos and the pictures and memorabilia from their trip to Ireland.

With a head full of shampoo lather oozing down the sides of her face, her hand groped to the shower valve to adjust the spray setting. But before her fingers touched the metal handle, a blast of scorching water made her yelp. She jerked the lever, lowering the temperature setting.

As the cooler water splashed over her body, her eyebrows bunched. What the heck? That hot water had gushed out before she'd even touched the handle. That shouldn't have happened.

Hannah had probably gotten up to use the other bathroom, causing the drop in cold water pressure. Rinsing the soap from her head, she decided that the water pressure probably needed a second look. They couldn't have this kind of thing happening if they had paying guests who would expect all the comforts of home. Why hadn't the home inspector picked up on that when they'd brought him in? Hopefully, he hadn't missed any other problems.

Finished in the bathroom, with her terry robe sashed, she entered the bedroom where Peter was just getting up. She leaned into him and planted a quick kiss. "Good morning! You're up early."

He blinked a few times as he rubbed the stubble on his cheeks, "I tried rolling over to go back to sleep but gave up when some car alarm went off. It sounded like it came from that house down the street where they're doing all those renovations."

Sharon went to the window and peeked out through the lace curtains. "Yeah, there're guys with tool belts unloading stuff from two vans there. That will be some place when they're finished. What a beautiful spot, right on the lake."

Peter mumbled as he headed to the bathroom, "The owner must be in some kind of hurry for them to be working on a Sunday. I'm sure there would involve serious overtime expenses."

Before she could mention the water pressure issue, the door to the bathroom snicked closed behind Peter. Oh, well. Hopefully, he'd have better luck than she had in the shower. She put her slippers on and left the room.

As she went down the gleaming oak stairs she smiled, glancing at the wall sconces lined up like tiered sentries. They were vintage, with an ornate brass base topped with amber, tulip-shaped lamps. They were charming set against the ivory

9

wall.

At the bottom of the staircase she plucked a stray flower petal from the table where an evening breeze must have disturbed the arrangement of red roses.

Closing her eyes, she inhaled the scent of fresh brewed coffee wafting from the kitchen. God bless modern technology and auto-timed coffee machines. The quiet of the morning settled like balm into her muscles as she poured herself a cup and added cream. On impulse, she took her coffee and headed to the sunroom to enjoy the vista of their yard and any birds that might be foraging for seed.

As she walked down the hall and through the family room, she looked over at the black TV monitor. She shuddered, remembering that fleeting touch on her cheek the night before. It had been unnerving in that late hour... But in the cool, clear air of morning, it was easy to put it down to imagination. Cocking her ear up the stairway, there was only silence above. Hannah was still asleep.

When she settled onto the wicker chaise, cupping the coffee in both hands, her shoulders shimmied feeling the soft kiss of an early morning breeze through the screens. This was the one indulgence she cherished, a few solitary moments alone starting the day. Give her that, and later she'd go through the house like a woman on a mission.

As she sipped the coffee, she acknowledged that Peter's and Hannah's teasing about her obsession for order and cleanliness was well earned. Even though there were only a few moving boxes left to unpack, she'd be glad when things were settled in their place.

From her perch next to the large screened windows she could look down on the yard ten feet below. A tangle of overgrown flowers almost obliterated the water flowing over a sheet of slate into the small pond. It was the focal point of the yard, resting beside a wide deck that led to the hot tub Peter and Hannah would work on later that day. With a bit of luck and elbow grease cleaning it, the three of them would enjoy an evening soak gazing at the stars.

The door to the sunroom popped open and Peter emerged carrying his own cup of Joe. "There you are." His bare feet padded against the painted floorboards, while a slight breeze parted his flannel robe revealing plaid boxers. He adjusted his housecoat and took a seat next to her.

"It sure is quiet... I mean aside from the noise down the street." He gazed at the perimeter of the enormous yard to the tall, privacy fence. "I'm glad that someone had the foresight to put that wooden fence up. A lot of the houses on this side of the street have backyards like fish bowls."

"For sure. We could weed the flowerbeds in our underwear and who would know?" She gazed over at him and took his free hand, "I know this is more of a commute for you to work, but you have to admit, it really is a beautiful place. With both kids gone, it'll be a beautiful home to retire in."

Peter sighed, "The kids leaving was bound to happen, although it's harder when it's the youngest." He brightened looking at her, "As for the drive, I guess it's my turn after your years on the road. Do you think you'll miss working for the Board of Ed?"

She snorted, "Not like there was much of a choice in staying on, not with the new government's requirements. Idiots. I'll take experience over a shiny new sheepskin degree any old day." It still rankled a bit being forced out even though she'd always had a dream of running her own business.

Forcing a smile, she continued, "I won't miss the bureaucracy, that's for sure. Or the white knuckle drive through blizzards and ice storms." She looked down into her mug of coffee, "I'll miss the kids though. Some of them really needed an advocate in their corner."

At her next thought, she blurted, "How was the water pressure and temperature in your shower? I almost got scalded rinsing my hair. I think maybe a toilet flushed and the drop in pressure—"

"No, that can't be. I was with the inspector when he checked it. He ran all the lines and flushed toilets to ensure the water pressure was consistent. I think you were taking measurements downstairs at the time. Everything was A-OK when he tested it."

"Well, I'm telling you the cold water pressure dropped when I was in the shower. I'm just worried about Hannah or guests getting scalded. We should have someone look at it. Maybe we need to get a supplemental pressure pump or something?"

Peter's eyebrows rose, and he nodded. "Okay. We'll call someone this week. But the town water comes from elevated towers. Being gravity based, the pressure should be consistent."

"Hmmm. Then the problem is in our house. I wonder if the previous owners ever had issues with the showers. Could it be a buildup of calcium? I could call her. Bonnie, I think that was her name. She left a number in all the house paperwork."

Sharon gazed out at a black bird who was taking a morning bath in the pond. "It was a shame the previous owners split up. They had everything set up for a B&B but it will be us who get to run it. I wonder what happened in their lives."

Peter stood up and reached for her mug, "I don't know, but it was strange. I mean... who leaves a house full of antique furniture? They would have done better financially if they'd sold it off separately, rather than include it in the sale."

She passed her mug to him and smiled, "Just one more and then I have to get moving. I'd like to make some blueberry muffins for Hannah before she gets up."

Peter mimicked looking at a non-existent wristwatch. "Oh, I think you've got plenty of time. It's three hours until noon. But nothing is stopping you from making them for me. I live here too."

"Just get me a coffee and then I'll think about it. Maybe." The smile she gave, looking up at him, would melt butter.

"If you want to use the hot tub tonight, you won't think too hard." He laughed as he opened the door to the family room. He stepped back and there was a puzzled look on his face, "Did you turn the TV monitor and my computer on? Were you searching for something on-line before I came down?"

Sharon's forehead tightened as she leaned toward him. "No. I came right out here, since it was such a beautiful morning. Why?"

When he turned to look into the corner of the room where the TV monitor was mounted, she rose to join him.

The monitor cast a bluish glow over the room. On the screen was a photo of Sharon and Peter standing under an arch of trees in a lane leading to a church. It was one they had taken in Ireland the year before, at St. Patrick's College Graveyard, in Kildare.

As she stood there staring, she felt a chill settle in the pit of her stomach. Somehow the monitor and computer had turned on while they'd been out in the sunroom having coffee. Hannah was still upstairs fast asleep, so how did the TV turn on?

She hesitated for a few moments before rushing over to check the power bar on the floor. The monitor plug was now plugged in, which made perfect sense. How else would the screen be lit up? The question was, who did it?

"This was unplugged when I went to bed, Peter. I distinctly remember checking it."

Peter shrugged. "Maybe Hannah had trouble sleeping last night. She must have come down here to watch a movie or something." He turned and went down the hallway to the kitchen.

Sharon stared at the picture displayed on the monitor before clicking the remote to turn it off. She'd check out Peter's theory when Hannah got up. But it was weird. Twice there'd been something funny going on with the monitor, not to mention that faint touch of something brushing her cheek. A shiver crept through her shoulders despite the warmth of the sun's rays filtering into the room.

She hurried out to join Peter in the kitchen. The peace of the morning sitting in the sunroom wasn't as appealing now.

THREE

A couple of hours later, with muffins made and pictures hung, Sharon sat down at the desk to tackle the job of creating a web page for the B&B. As the laptop booted up, she looked around at the small nook where she had set the file cabinet and printer. It was a section of the master bedroom ideal for her office, with a bank of windows on two sides, allowing a slice of the lake to be seen between the rooftops of houses across the street.

She turned to the screen and entered her password. Just as the window opened to the web page she had started, the thuds of fast footsteps coming up the stairs caught her attention.

Hannah bounded into the room wearing a mile-wide grin along with her blue pajamas. "Okay. Where is it?" Without waiting for an answer, she raced to the king-sized bed and went to her knees, peering under it.

Sharon rose slowly, staring at her daughter. "Where is what? What are you looking for, sweetie?"

Hannah bounced up and sprinted to the curtains, pulling them back to peer at the floor. "Come on, Mom! I know you got me a kitten. You're trying to make sure I spend as much time as possible out here visiting you and Dad. The kitten is the clincher." She smiled, hurrying to the door of the ensuite bathroom.

Sharon's mouth fell open, watching her. Hannah had always wanted a cat, but thankfully she'd never pushed the issue. With their work schedules, each of them gone for most of the day, having an animal wouldn't be fair.

Hannah stepped out of the bathroom and folded her arms over her chest, still grinning like the Cheshire Cat. "I know you got me a kitten for my birthday. Where did you stash it, Mom?" The young teen slapped her forehead and exclaimed, "Dad! He's got it."

As she was about to run out of the bedroom in search of her father, Sharon called out to her. "No, Hannah. I'm sorry to tell you this, but we didn't get a cat for you for your birthday." She thought of the expensive leather jacket she'd got for Hannah and sighed. She should have saved the money. A cat would have been more appreciated by her daughter.

Hannah stopped short and peered at her. "You're telling me the truth? There's no kitten?" Her face tightened, and she scratched her head. "Then what's with the toilet paper in my bathroom? It's strewn everywhere, from the holder out to the hall and all through my bedroom."

"What? What do you mean it's strewn everywhere? That doesn't make sense." Sharon stepped over to Hannah, watching her closely. Was her daughter pulling some kind of prank?

Hannah grabbed Sharon's wrist. "Come on. I'll show you." Hannah pulled Sharon down the hallway to the door leading to the other section of the house. "You really didn't get me a cat? I looked all over downstairs and figured it had come up to your room." Before they stepped through the doorway, Hannah's eyes narrowed, pinning her mother with a pointed look. "You're sure? No cat?"

Sharon let out an exasperated sigh. "No cat. God's truth. Now what the heck—"

"Holy shit." Hannah let go of her mother and stepped into

the short hallway. "Who did this, then?"

Sharon's eyes opened wider when she joined her. A white trail of toilet paper lay in loops at her feet, branching off with one path leading to the bathroom and the other to Hannah's bedroom. She glanced at Hannah and then back to the lines of tissue. "Come on now. You did this, Hannah. You're playing a trick on me."

Hannah's voice became softer, and she shook her head. "No, Mom. I didn't. I just got up, and this is exactly how I found everything. Honest."

Sharon walked over to the bathroom door and pushed it open wider. Toilet paper rolled up the side of the tub and circled round the faucet before draping over the lip of the tub. Barely even breathing, she followed the paper trail down the two steps into Hannah's bedroom. It ran helter-skelter around the room, in small heaps near the bedside table, under the lamp and then flowing out the door to the stairs.

The only person who could have done this was Peter. But why? If this was supposed to be funny, it was not even remotely amusing.

"Hey! What's with the toilet paper? Are you up, Hannah?" Peter's footsteps thudded softly on the set of stairs leading to Hannah's room. When he stepped through the entrance, he held a loose wad of tissue in his hand. His gaze ricocheted between Sharon and his daughter. "What's going on?"

Sharon scooped up the paper near her, resisting the urge to snap at him when she answered, "I was going to ask you the same thing. Why would you leave a mess like this in Hannah's bath and her room? Is this supposed to be funny, Peter? April Fool's Day isn't for another eight months."

"You think *I* did this? Why would I make a mess like this?" He snatched up more paper as he made his way closer.

"Did you get me a cat, Dad? Kind of a surprise for me and going behind Mom's back? Please tell me you got me a cat, Dad." Hannah hugged her body, running her hands up her upper arms. The tendons in her neck were tight like piano strings.

Sharon swallowed the words that threatened to leap off her tongue. The kid looked kind of freaked out. Okay, it wasn't Peter, so it had to be Hannah who did this. But why? Had she done this in her sleep? Some sleep-walking episode? If she had, it would have been the first time she'd ever done that.

Peter scooped up the last of the paper in the bedroom and turned to Hannah. "I wish I'd got you a cat, Hannah. At least we'd know what made this mess."

Seeing the fright in Hannah's eyes, Sharon spoke quickly, "Maybe an animal got in last night. It could have been a squirrel or—"

"Don't say rat, Mom. I swear if you say rat, I'm going out right now and getting a cat. I don't care what you say." Hannah squeezed her eyes shut as she shuddered.

Sharon let out another sigh before stepping into the bathroom to get the rest of the mess cleaned up. She snapped off what was left of the roll from the holder and straightened. As she passed the mirror hanging over the vanity she jerked back.

In the corner of her vision she'd seen something dark flit across the glass. She leaned closer, peering at the mirror with narrow eyes. It had been just a fraction of a second that she'd seen it—a shadow that moved fast.

Her heart beat faster as she continued examining the mirror. Had there really been something in the glass? She glanced at the window where the light from the day outside burst through. Maybe a cloud had passed over and caused a momentary darkness. But the feeling that had hit her the night before in the family room flooded through her once more. She'd seen a glimpse of something in that mirror. Plus, who the hell had strewn toilet paper all over Hannah's room?

She took a deep breath and continued swiping toilet paper from the tub and floor.

A cloud might have caused the movement she'd seen in the mirror. As for the toilet paper mess, it had to be Hannah, or some animal got in. But Hannah had never, ever stirred from her bed when she'd gone to sleep for the night. Even as a toddler, she had been the best baby to sleep through. Now, if it was her son, Spencer, then maybe yes. He'd been more challenging, often curling up between her and Peter in the middle of the night. But not Hannah.

She bumped right into Peter when he appeared in the doorway. "Sorry."

He took the sheaves of tissue from her and balled everything into a tight wad. "There has to be a cat or something that got in the house. I'll check the basement to see if there's a broken window or if there's a way in for animals. The people who lived here before had a cat. Hell, they even put a 'cat door' in the porch. Maybe the cat had a friend who liked to visit, or god forbid there's a litter of kittens stashed somewhere."

"If you find a litter, I get to keep one! It's only fair after all this."

Peter rolled his eyes at Hannah and then continued, "After I check the house I'll go to the hardware store to see if they have any live traps. It could be a squirrel or raccoon."

Sharon nodded. "You're right. That has to be it." She smiled at Hannah, "Hate to break it to you but the only cat you're getting will be the one you buy for your own home. I like cats as long as they belong to other people."

"Mo....om." Hannah's shoulders drooped, and she flopped down on the bed.

"Save the acting for the theatre, sweetie. No cats." Sharon patted her daughter's arm as she followed Peter from the room. Ugh. Cats. Just more hair to vacuum, not to mention a messy litter box to deal with. But at least a cat would explain the toilet paper caper.

As she was about to leave the room she paused and looked back at Hannah, "Did you unplug the TV monitor last night before you went to bed?"

"No. Why?"

She watched Hannah closely. "It was unplugged when I checked it last night, but was plugged back in this morning. I just figured you may have done that. And you slept well? No getting up to watch a movie or create that mess with the toilet paper?"

"No! What the heck, Mom? What are you talking about?"

"We'll check the house. It had to be a cat or squirrel or something." She hurried from the room before Hannah could say anything more about anything.

For sure there were strange things going on, but there had to be some kind of logical explanation. She couldn't let herself jump to conclusions; the last thing she would do was delve into things she experienced as a child. That part of her life ended long ago.

The home was beautiful, everything she had ever dreamt about owning. Even the village was charming with the old homes and over-sized lots, bordered by two bodies of water. Moving to a new house usually took some getting used to. There had to be a reason for all the odd stuff going on.

Still, as she walked down the stairs to the family room, her gaze scoured the area. Looking for... She stopped in her tracks. What the heck *was* she looking for? The TV was black and everything was in order. No touches on her cheek or sudden electricity surge.

So why did the fine hairs on the back of her neck prickle? She shivered and hurried into the kitchen to start lunch.

FOUR

Twenty minutes later, while Sharon set the table, the basement door opened, and Peter appeared.

She paused for a moment and tried to read his face. But the shrug of his shoulders told her they were no closer to solving the mystery of the toilet paper trail than before.

As he passed by her to wash his hands in the sink, he muttered, "Everything is fine down there; no broken windows or sign of any animal. There's no shortage of dust and yucky cobwebs, though."

Sighing, she set the napkins beside the plates. "An animal getting in is the only logical explanation, Peter. There has to be some way in that you missed."

"Well, even if I missed it and a cat or squirrel got into the basement, how could it get through that door closing off the basement?" Peter turned from the sink and met Sharon's gaze. "Mice might find a way in. Maybe I should pick some mousetraps up when I go to the store."

Sharon shook her head. "I don't think a mouse would be capable of doing that mess in Hannah's bathroom. Remember, the paper was even draped over the bathtub. Mice can't climb porcelain."

Hannah entered the kitchen and took a seat at the table. "So what's the verdict? Did you find anything?"

Even though Hannah's tone was casual, it was obvious from the way she perched on the edge of her seat, hands clasped tightly together, that it worried her. Sharon lifted a lock of hair from her daughter's cheek and tucked it behind her ear, before giving Hannah's shoulder a gentle squeeze.

"Your father didn't see anything, but I'll look as well. No offense, Peter, but sometimes a second set of eyes helps. Plus, if it's a cat getting in, my nose will pick up on that, especially if they're spraying. I think your first thought that it was a cat was probably right, Hannah. It's the only thing that makes any sense."

Hannah grimaced before getting up to open the fridge. "I'll help you, Mom. But can we eat first? I'm starving."

Sharon looked over at Peter, trying to gauge his thoughts. But if he was perplexed about the issue with the toilet paper, he gave no sign of it, as he carried the plate of sandwiches and a jug of milk to the table. Or maybe he was trying to downplay it in front of Hannah.

"Aha! I knew I smelled baking!" Hannah took the plastic box filled with blueberry muffins to the table and set them next to her.

Sharon sat down across from her and smiled, trying to lighten the mood. "I was up bright and early so I baked them for you. Not to mention hanging pictures and starting my website. I've been busy."

Peter poured milk for Hannah and then sat down next to her. "You still up for helping me with the hot tub? We can do that after I get back from the hardware store."

"Sure. I'd rather be outside, anyway." Hannah bit into the muffin.

Sharon's gaze shot to her daughter, but it didn't look like there was any hidden meaning in her comment, like she was still worried about the toilet paper incident. No, it was probably more a reflection of being cooped up in a bakery for most of the week and needing to get outside.

Perhaps it was only she who was still thinking about the odd things that had happened since they'd moved in. If that was the case then she needed to get past it. It was an unfamiliar house to them. A book slipping onto the remote could have caused the blaring monitor. As for the monitor being unplugged, maybe she herself had done it. Because it was such an unconscious thing to do, she couldn't recall specifically doing it. Or not doing it. It wouldn't be the first time she'd gone on auto pilot forgetting things.

It was her age. When she was a young mother, she remembered older women talking about 'the change'. Well, now she was going through menopause herself and it was anything but fun with the hot flashes and memory lapses, to say nothing of emotional highs and lows.

She shook her head ruefully. It was puberty in reverse.

"Sharon? Hey, earth to Sharon."

She startled at Peter's words, blinking at him. "What? Sorry, I was lost in thought. What did you say?"

"I asked if there was anything else you need while I'm out shopping?" There was a hint of unease in his face even though he smiled at her. "Are you okay, Shar?"

"Yes! I was just daydreaming. Is that a crime?" Seeing the hurt in his eyes, her tone softened. "I'm sorry. Actually, could you pick up sixty watt LED light bulbs? I noticed the lights in the family room flickering yesterday. They should be switched from incandescent to save energy, anyway."

"Sure! I'm all over saving money, right? I hate to leave you with the clean-up but I want to get this done so we can start the work outside." He rose to his feet and took his plate to the sink.

"I'll help Mom with cleaning up." Hannah gave her father a slight shove as he walked by her. "Just go, Dad, so we can get that hot tub up and running."

"I know when I'm not wanted. I can take a hint."

The chuckle that followed Peter's remark as he walked down the hallway to leave struck Sharon as too light. Like her, he was trying to downplay everything that had happened for Hannah's sake—at least until they found a reasonable explanation.

"If you finish in here, Hannah, I'll go downstairs to double check everything." Sharon looked over at her daughter who was piling the few plates into the dishwasher.

"Okay. I want to throw some things in the washing machine so they're ready for work this week. I'll be down in five minutes, Mom."

Sharon reached for the flashlight before opening the door leading to the basement. The basement was actually more of a cellar because of the age of the house, but it was dry with a cement floor. The second step creaked as she stepped down and flipped the light switch on.

Her gaze darted past the washer and dryer to the far recesses of the enormous room. Two pairs of ice skates and a roll of heavy duty electrical extension looped from hooks sticking from the main support beam of the house. She stepped down the last step onto the cement pad and made her way to the far wall where faint light from a tiny window filtered down over a set of shelves.

When a cob web fluttering from the beam overhead brushed her hair, she immediately swept it away with a shudder. Ugh. Peter had been right about that. No shortage of spiders down there. She flicked the light of her flashlight on to examine the edges of the window for any sign of an opening. Aside from years of dust and husks of dead insects, it was secured around the outside edges.

Shining the beam to the other limestone wall of the basement, she crept over to that area, aiming the beam to inspect it for crevices.

"Mom?"

She jerked back, hearing Hannah's voice coming from the top of the stairs. As her daughter's feet peppered down the stairs, Sharon exhaled slowly. "Over here, Hannah."

"Did you find anything yet?" The bang of the washing machine lid against the control panel followed as Hannah started her laundry.

"Nothing so far."

The water rushing into the washing machine and the closing of the lid was a backdrop as Sharon ran her hand over the cool stone wall. As she stepped away to examine another section, a thundering bang above her head made her jerk back.

"Mom? What was that?" Hannah raced over to her mother's side, abandoning the laundry.

Sharon's heart was in her throat as she stared at the ceiling of the cellar. There was no one home but them, unless Peter had returned. But that made little sense; he'd just left!

Sharon gasped and Hannah yelped when the cellar lights went out. Dark shadowy gloom filled the area, as the only light was from her flashlight and the filthy basement window on the opposite wall.

Hannah clutched her mother, her fingers digging into her arm. "Mom? What was that bang? What's with the light going out?" She whispered so close to Sharon's ear that her breath was warm on Sharon's face.

"Peter? Is that you?" With Hannah still clinging to her arm, Sharon led the way towards the stairway. The beam of light before her wavered in her shaking hand even though she tried hard to remain calm. One thing she was certain of, was that Peter would not make that much of a crash without announcing his presence.

Again that tingly feeling crept through her shoulders. This was beyond weird. The only other explanation was that someone had entered their house. But why had the lights gone off?

Reaching the bottom stair, she shone the flashlight up and froze. The heavy wooden door was shut tight. That had to be the banging she'd heard.

"Mo....om. What the heck?" Hannah clutched her arm tighter. "We're locked down here in the dark?"

"No." She looked over at Hannah, seeing her own fright mirrored in her daughter's face. "I mean, we don't know that it's locked. C'mon. Let's get out of here." She started up the steps. Her palm was sweaty, gripping the railing for dear life.

"Mom? The washing machine stopped. All the power is out down here."

Sharon kept climbing up the stairs, trying to keep her voice even. "It's got to be a fuse, Hannah. We'll get the door open and then we can check that."

When her fingers grabbed the door handle, Sharon's mouth fell open. The damned door was locked! She tried turning it both ways, but the knob would not budge. Her heart pounded like a racehorse and it was suddenly hard to breathe. The walls of the narrow stairway pressed down on her while Hannah hugged into her back.

"Why won't it open, Mom? Someone locked it? We're trapped here! Oh God!" Hannah's voice had become higher pitched, like a frightened child's.

"Maybe a breeze caught it and made it slam shut." She tried the knob once more before banging on it with her fist. "Peter?"

"I don't like this. I'm scared, Mom."

Sharon turned and pulled Hannah into her, hugging her tightly. "We'll be okay, Hannah. Your father will be home from the store soon and he'll let us out. We just have to be patient." But the calm she tried to project into her words didn't resonate in her own mind. They had a flashlight and each other, but that was all.

"What is with this house? There's something weird here, Mom. First the toilet paper and now this?"

She rubbed her daughter's back and pulled her closer still. But she felt anything but confident in the dark cellar stairwell. There was also the TV monitor turning on by itself and blaring last night. Then there was the thing unplugging and then plugging it in again. Not to mention the touch on her skin and the photo on the screen. Those were things she would not point out to her daughter. No. Way.

"Shhh. Do you hear that?" Sharon tilted her head to the side, listening hard. Had that been a car door just now? The sound of her heartbeat threatened to drown out any other sound, and she held her breath.

"Yes! He's back!" She pounded on the door with her palm. Hannah wasted no time in adding to the banging on the locked door.

They almost fell forward onto the floor before them when the door swung open. Peter caught Sharon's arm, steadying her and his daughter.

"What happened? What are you doing?"

Sharon's hand fluttered to her chest, and she took a deep breath. "The door slammed shut, and it locked."

Peter's face knotted with worry lines. "That door wasn't locked, Shar. The deadbolt is off and that's the only way it locks."

She stared at the edge of the door. The deadbolt was tucked into the door and its lever was set in the 'unlock' position. She scrambled for the doorknob, gripping it tightly. It turned easily in her hand. Oh, my god. That couldn't be. She'd been unable to turn the doorknob at all!

"No Dad! It was definitely locked! I was there. I saw Mom trying to get the door open." Hannah stepped by her parents, going into the kitchen. "The window is only open a crack. No wind could have caused that door to shut and especially not when it slammed so hard. It closed on its own and it locked."

Sharon saw the fear in her daughter's wide eyes and the blanched color of her face. Although she herself was still shaken from the horror of being trapped, she knew that she had to put up a brave front for Hannah. "Peter, will you check the house to make sure no one came in? Why did we get locked us down there?"

Peter nodded. "You two stay here. I'll check upstairs." He strode out of the room and his feet pounded fast up the stairs in the front of the house.

Hannah's hands were tight to her chest when she darted to her mother's side. "Mom, I don't think he will find anyone. There's something weird going on in this house and it's not an intruder. Maybe that's why the previous owners left."

Sharon shook her head. "No. They were going through a

divorce. They went their separate ways and left everything behind." When she saw Hannah roll her eyes, she added, "But it wouldn't hurt to call them and find out if they ever experienced odd things here." At this point she wasn't ready to have an open discussion on this, at least not with Hannah.

Her stomach was a tight knot recalling all the strange, inexplicable things that had happened since they'd moved in. It was hard groping for logical explanations when she was unnerved by it all.

"This place is creepy. I think it's haunted, Mom. Someone doesn't want us here. They probably drove the previous owners out."

Sharon was spared arguing the point when Peter entered the kitchen again.

"I checked every room upstairs and the family room. There's only us here." He walked over to the basement door and opened it wider, watching to see if it shut on its own. "Maybe it isn't hung properly, so it's always inclined to swing shut."

But the door never moved an iota from where he'd left it open. He shut it softly and turned to Sharon. "Okay that's not the reason. There's no one besides us, here. So how did that door bang shut?"

"How did the toilet paper get strewn all over the bathroom and my room? Why did the TV blare on last night?" Hannah directed her questions at Sharon. From the set of her jaw, she dared her mother to explain those things away.

Sharon's gaze darted between Peter and Hannah, her mind scrambling to come up with some reasonable answer. Hannah had made a good point. Plus, there were the odd feelings which she had experienced.

With all the weird things happening, how could she and Peter live there? And forget Hannah ever wanting to visit. Why would she, when the place was so freaking odd? Sharon could see her dream of opening up a bed and breakfast circling the drain. If the house was haunted could they ever expect guests to stay for even a night?

No.

That would not happen. This place was perfect for everything she wanted to do with the rest of her life.

"Look." She held her hands up to silence her husband and daughter. "I don't know why these things are happening. We need to investigate the history of this house, talk to the former owners. If, in the worst case scenario, the house is haunted, we un-haunt it."

"What?" Peter's stared at her incredulously. "You can't be serious about that, Sharon. You think the house is *haunted*?"

Ignoring Peter's outburst Sharon continued, "There must be something we can do to make this a normal house! In the meantime, let's take stock. There's been some weird crap going on. I won't deny that. But none of us has actually been harmed." It was a weak argument, and she wasn't surprised when Hannah countered.

"Harmed? Being scared out of my skin downstairs, locked in a dark basement, didn't harm me? The toilet paper thing? I'll never sleep tonight, Mom."

"You could take the room next to ours, Hannah, if that helps."

"Get me a kitten. That might help, Dad." Hannah smiled sheepishly at her father. "Seriously. I'm more worried about you guys than me. I'm out of here tomorrow and back in Kingston, but *you* live here. What if I'm right and this place is haunted?"

Sharon sensed a weakening in Hannah's position which was an opening to get past this, at least until they had more things to go on. "Well I say, set the traps you bought, Peter. I will do some digging on the background of the house and see what we can find out."

"Sounds like a plan, Shar. My money is on a four legged intruder, though. Just sayin'. "Peter scooped up the live trap he had abandoned in the hallway and opened the door to the basement wider.

Sharon handed the flashlight to him. "You'd better check the breaker panel, Peter. The lights and washing machine went out when we were down there. I'll find something to prop this door open so it won't bang shut on you when you're down there."

She grabbed a tea towel from the cabinet and stuffed it in the crack between the floor and the edge of the door. When she straightened, she looked over at Hannah. "I'll finish your laundry. You get dressed and by that time your father will be ready to start the yard work."

Without waiting for an answer, Sharon went into the kitchen to get some cheese to bait the live trap that Peter had bought. Hannah's footsteps could be heard going up the stairs when Sharon stepped through the doorway to join Peter.

She stood at the landing for a few moments, taking deep breaths to settle her nerves. The downstairs was still dark and she could hear Peter opening the panel to flip the breaker. When the light in the basement went on and the washing machine whirred to life, she squared her shoulders and walked down the stairs.

Trying hard to remain confident, she helped Peter with the trap. All the while, the dim recesses in the corners of the room made her glance over her shoulder more than a few times. With the trap set and Hannah's laundry looked after, she breathed a sigh of relief before going up the stairs again.

One thing she knew for sure...she had to get to the bottom of what was causing the weird things happening in her house. There would be many days ahead when she would be on her own, alone in this place. She had to figure this out and fix it if her dream of living here would ever come about.

But somewhere deep in the recesses of her brain, there was unease. This was too reminiscent of her childhood.

The part of her childhood she kept tucked away in the back room of her memories.

Was it happening again?

FIVE

Later that afternoon, Sharon rifled through boxes of legal papers set out in the cozy nook in her bedroom. Her laptop yawned open on the antique roll-top desk tucked under the windows. Beside it was a filing cabinet. She paused for a moment to gaze out the large windows framing the area. It was possible to see the blue of Big Rideau Lake between the houses lining the street below. The quiet beauty of the scene made the earlier events in the home seem surreal.

But they had happened. There was no getting around that fact.

With a drawn out sigh, she grabbed the legal folder from the top of the first box to sort through the papers to label them and place them into proper file jackets. These were papers that she and Peter had received from the lawyer, the bank and insurance company which she had already read through. As she was sorting through them, two documents caught her eye. Pitted and yellowed with age, they were unlike the other papers.

Her eyebrows drew together as she examined them. She'd been through this file a couple times since the closing of the sale and never saw these papers before. The first paper was an ancient handwritten list of all the owners who had at one time laid claim to the property, listing the seller, the buyer, the date of transfer all the way back to the 1800's. The second sheet was also handwritten but it appeared more like a letter or journal entry. Even the page showed faint lines like in it was from a notebook.

> To whoever finds this...
> To most folks around here, Liam Gallagher was thought to be a drinker, a gambler and a prankster. He was all of that, but he was also a loving father. I would know, as he was my Dad.
> The last Halloween of my father's life is one which will haunt me till my dying day. It was the first dance which I ever went to at the school. Dad took Eve and me there in our automobile. It was the last time that I ever saw my dad alive.
> Liam Gallagher was found the next day in the lake, drowned (near fountain). Foul play was suspected, but no one was ever charged with the crime.
> R~~

Sharon reread the cryptic note. The signature of the offspring who had written it was almost incomprehensible except for the first letter, an 'R'. She read the note a second time. This Liam Gallagher had drowned and his child had written this strange note about it. As tragic as that was, it didn't explain how the note was now in their documents.

She scanned the other aged paper, a handwritten list detailing all the owners of the property and dates of sales. Near the bottom was Liam Gallagher's name and his wife Ginny listed as purchasing the property in 1940. The next entry was the sale in 1953, handled by Sean Gallagher, Executor. Liam Gallagher had once lived in this home, with his wife and children, before coming to a tragic end.

Sharon's hand trembled as she gazed at the two papers.

There was no way that these pages had been with the other legal documents she and Peter had gone through the day before. Sure, they'd been pretty excited about acquiring the property, but the two yellowed documents were really old. They would have stood out, especially handwritten, and with such a dire story. Nope. It wasn't likely that both she and Peter would have missed it.

That left only one explanation. Someone had put the note and the ownership record in that file *after* they'd looked through them. But who would do that? Even more puzzling was why someone would go to the trouble of slipping them in with the legal papers.

Finding the two papers felt the same as when the door to the basement slammed shut and the toilet paper strewn over Hannah's area of the house. That same tingling feeling that she'd experienced the night before at the gossamer brush on her cheek, that tingling sensation that brought back in full force the memory of seeing her grandmother was like a weight holding her in the chair. She swallowed hard.

Hannah's comment that the house was haunted was spot on.

She was *meant* to see these two papers. Sharon's heartbeat fluttered faster and her breath froze in her chest. Whatever or whoever had caused the creepy things that had happened in the house wanted her to know more. Her face was tight when she reread the first line of the note.

... Liam Gallagher was a drinker, a gambler and a prankster.

A prankster. The toilet paper being strewn over the bathroom and Hannah's room could qualify as a prank. Even the TV monitor blaring the night before and finding the photo from Ireland on the screen could at a stretch be called a prank. Getting locked in the basement and unplugging and then plugging the monitor back in was definitely not funny though. No. That had been scary. Okay, scary and frightening…but a *prank*.

Like a small electric current, that tingling feeling furled up her spine to the top of her head in a series of waves. She knew that sensation well. She hadn't had it in a long, long time, but those ripples up her back were familiar. They were just like the times when she was a child.

Sharon's mind tripped to a time many years ago. She saw her father's face giving her hell when she hid his car keys. He was angry that he'd be late for work. But for days, she'd had dreams of a fiery accident at the intersection he had to pass through to get to his job at the factory. He had to take a taxi that day, and he was an hour later than usual in leaving the house. But it was when she was riding the school bus that her blood had turned cold. There had been a terrible accident with two cars at the intersection before the factory. It had happened earlier around the time that her father would normally be on his way to work. If not for hiding his keys, it would have involved him.

But it wasn't just the dreams. There was that odd fluttery feeling in her head, kind of a dizzy sensation, every time she had looked at her father in the days before. Both things combined had bothered her so much that she knew she had to stop him from being anywhere near that intersection that morning. When he got home from work that night, he forgot her punishment. His face had been ashen telling her that if not for her, he would have been in that multiple vehicle smash-up.

She closed her eyes and tried to shake the memory off. It was happening again. The 'curse', as she used to call it, along with the fluttery thing, was happening again. Why now? Was it because of the house? She set the papers on her desk and stood up, her gaze scanning over the room. Was this Liam guy, who had died mysteriously, in the room with her now?

The thumps of footsteps on the stairs made her gasp, jerking back.

Peter stepped into the room. "Hey, that bed of daylilies behind the pond—" When he got a look at Sharon, he stopped short. "What's wrong? You look like—"

"I found some papers, Peter." She reached for the yellowed papers and handed them to her husband. "I was filing our documents away and came across these. I've never seen these before. You don't remember seeing these in the set of legal papers, do you?" Even though she asked, she knew the answer would be no.

He scanned the ledger before reading the letter written by 'R'. His eyebrows arched when he looked back at Sharon. "Nope. These weren't in the papers we looked through yesterday. You just found them?"

She nodded quickly. "Yeah. You know what I'm thinking? I was *meant* to find them. There are some strange things happening in this house, Peter, and now these papers show up."

Peter inhaled deeply and let it out slowly. "Things have been odd. But now you're sounding like Hannah. You can't seriously think that this house is haunted."

"Why *wouldn't* I think that? Do you have a better explanation? I didn't tell you this before, but I felt something touch my cheek when I was in the family room last night. I put it down to fatigue or my imagination, but now I don't think that was it. It gave me the willies."

"Something touched you?" He stared at her silently for a few beats. "Look. I'll admit that the TV monitor showing our photo this morning and that complete mess with the toilet paper kind of freaked me out. But I'm not willing to buy into some haunting theory like you and Hannah."

"You think I like the fact that my home may be haunted? Believe me, that's the last thing I need right now. How can I have guests in my home when they may wake up to the mess of toilet paper or the TV blaring? But it isn't just the business I'm worried about. This is... well, scary, you know?"

"Maybe you could use the odd stuff as a marketing tool." He smiled to let her know he was joking before he continued, "Some people are really into that haunted stuff."

She snatched the papers from his hands, "Well, I'm not. Not in my home, trying to set up a business!" She didn't add that she'd had more than her share of unexplainable events in her life when she was a child. As far as Peter knew, she'd seen her dead grandmother, and that was it. Premonitions and that fuzzy feeling had stopped long before she'd met Peter.

Her eyes flashed at her next thought. "We can't tell Hannah about these papers. She's already worried that the house is haunted. She will never want to come out to visit us!"

"Earth to Sharon! She's already convinced the place is haunted! But you're right. Until we know for sure what's going on, we should keep finding these papers to ourselves." Peter shrugged, "With any luck that may be the last of it. If you're right that you were meant to see that Liam Gallagher owned this house, and that he may have been murdered... maybe that's enough. Perhaps he will be vindicated with that and leave us alone."

Sharon nodded. "I hope so."

She slipped the papers into a file jacket and grabbed a pen to label it. When she was through, she stood up. "Hannah will wonder what's taking you so long. I'll come down and see about the daylilies near the pond."

"I left her scrubbing the hot tub. That will take at least twenty minutes. But yeah, we'd better go down." Peter pulled Sharon into a one-armed hug, kissing her forehead, "I'll defer to your decision about telling Hannah about this."

He flashed a nervous grin, looking down at her as they walked from the bedroom, "Why wouldn't he haunt the lake instead of here? That's where he died. That makes more sense to me."

Sharon could only stare at her husband. Of the two of them, he would be the one more likely to be spooked by the fact that odd things were happening. She remembered Peter's brother Carl, telling the story of how he scared the daylights out of Peter, skulking outside near a window after they'd watched a scary movie. Yet he didn't seem bothered by what was happening right there in their home. Or maybe he was and didn't want to add to her worries.

Looking away from Peter and up to the ceiling, she said, "I don't know why he'd haunt this house rather than where he drowned. So far, it seems the ghost is more preoccupied with me than with you." Sharon followed Peter down the stairs.

"The letter said he was a prankster," Peter mulled. "There certainly have been pranks, although I don't find his sense of humor all that funny."

"The poor man was murdered if that note is correct. Not only that, but if he's still here haunting this house, it's going to be difficult to live here, let alone operate a B&B. Hannah's not the only one spooked by this, Peter."

When Peter turned to her, his tone was stern. "What really bugs me is this Liam character turning my electrical stuff on and running my hydro bills up. And...he's not even a paying guest. That's just not fair."

Sharon gave him a slight jab with her elbow. "Not funny, Peter. It's not the money, it's the fact that he shouldn't be here. He doesn't belong in our lives or this house."

As they walked down the stairs, the wall sconce lights flickered a few times. Sharon's jaw dropped, and she stood stock-still watching the lights.

The smile that had been on Peter's face fell like dirt dropping onto an open grave. "Okay. I agree, playing with our lights isn't funny." He peered at the wall sconces and then gave a pointed look at Sharon, "You know that could also be a loose wire or connection. It wouldn't hurt to get an electrician in to double-check everything. As for those papers we found, it is possible that those letters were there and in our excitement, we didn't notice them."

Sharon was certain that those papers hadn't been there when they'd first gone through the bundle. But there was no point in arguing it. They were there now, and they now had a better idea of who they were dealing with. She sighed. They had bought the perfect place to realize her dream, to run her own business. There had to be some way of getting rid of this spirit if he continued plaguing them with his tricks.

She followed Peter through the dining room to enter the kitchen. "Okay. Maybe getting an electrician in is a good idea. If nothing else, it will rule out that explanation. Although I'm not convinced." That old fluttery feeling in the back of her mind was telling her that logic couldn't explain what was happening in her home.

As they walked through the family room to go outside, Sharon examined each area with narrow eyes. What was the next prank their ghostly resident would scare them with?

SIX

For the next half hour they busied themselves with sorting through the perennial flowers, deciding which to keep and which to move to another location. Even though she'd busied herself in the gardening, the note and the other creepy stuff played in the back recesses of her mind. Plus, she didn't want to upset Hannah any more with any speculation while she'd been working beside them.

When Hannah went back inside to put the cleaning supplies away, Sharon turned to Peter, "According to the letter, Liam was also a gambler. Could it be that there was a dispute when he was playing poker and someone pushed him into the lake?"

Peter dry scrubbed his hands over his face. "You're still thinking about this."

"Ya think?" How could she *not* be thinking about this?

"Honey, have you considered that the note might not even be correct? Who knows if it wasn't written by some bored teenager trying to be dramatic? I'm sure that there was a Liam Gallagher who lived here, but being drowned because of a prank or cheating at cards? That's certainly not worth killing someone over. This might be Westport's version of an urban legend."

With arms akimbo, she leaned into him, "I'm going to do some research on Liam Gallagher. Surely there are old newspaper clippings in the public library. If someone drowned him, then there'd be a police report, wouldn't there? His drowning would have made the local paper."

"For what it's worth, maybe you're right." He smiled as he looked down at her. "It'd be a damned sight cheaper living with a ghost than rewiring the entire house! We just have to get him to stay out of the bathrooms and leave our electricity alone."

She laughed and shook her head. "Mr. Cheapskate. You squeeze a nickel so hard that you make it yelp! You've probably still have the first dollar you ever earned... framed!"

"It was a quarter from picking strawberries for old Mrs. Judd and yes, I still have it." He turned when the screen door slammed.

Hannah came down the steps and joined them on the small deck. She pulled her strawberry blonde locks up into a ponytail as she spoke, "The hot tub is filling as we speak."

Peter smirked, "Nice to see you're earning your keep. Next up, weeding and transplanting some flowers around the pond."

"Da...ad!" Hannah smirked "I don't have to earn my keep. You're lucky to be blessed with a daughter like me!"

"And so modest!" Peter tugged her ponytail when she turned, heading over to the bed of flowers.

Sharon smiled, seeing the easy banter between them. If Hannah was still upset about the morning's escapades, she was doing a good job of hiding it. She left the two of them and went back into the house to finish organizing her office space. Her gaze darted to the wall sconce lights as she walked up the stairs. Thankfully, everything was quiet, no flickering on or off.

When she rounded the corner entering the bedroom, she stopped short. "Oh my God..." The room looked like a tornado had blasted through it! Grasping the door frame to steady herself, that same dizzy, tingling feeling flooded through her as she gaped at the office space.

The box of files and legal documents was overturned. Papers were strewn all over the desk and floor! She swallowed hard, seeing the yellowed letter and the title document laying on top of the heap, perfectly centered.

Her heart hammered hard and fast in her throat as she stood rooted to the spot. This was definitely real—a haunting. Something had lifted those boxes and turned them upside down. Even though paper was scattered all over her desk, that the old letter and document topping the pile was another message meant for her.

Wait. Not something. Someone.

Liam Gallagher wanted her to know it was him and that he was here to stay.

SEVEN

Backing out slowly, she spun around at the newel post of the stairs. Her feet flew on the steps and she raced across the dining room to the front door. It was only when she was outside on the front veranda that she paused, gulping air. Her hand shook when she reached to grip the railing. There was definitely a ghost haunting in their home. This Liam character was making a statement to let her know he was there.

She sank down on the front step, willing her heart to slow. But all the while she kept seeing in her mind's eye the mess she'd encountered in her office area. This wasn't just a prank like the scattered toilet paper. She could sense frustration... even anger in how her papers and boxes were tossed over the office area. The hairs on the back of her neck spiked high.

There was no way she was going back in there alone. Peter had to see what had happened. Maybe then he would believe that the house was haunted. It wasn't just an electrical issue or some animal creating havoc. It was this Liam guy!

It took a good twenty minutes for her heartbeat to resume its normal pace. She wiped a bead of sweat from her brow, trying to compose herself. As if the scary mess upstairs wasn't enough, a hot flash? Shit.

She and Peter needed to figure out how to deal with this. That trip to the library would include research on getting rid of a ghost as well as finding out more about Liam Gallagher.

As she walked down the steps to the front flower beds, she murmured, "Not funny, Liam. Definitely not a funny prank."

***

As tempting as it was to go around to the back of the house to get Peter to show him the mess that had been left in her bedroom office, she resisted. She busied herself weeding the front flower beds, trying to calm down before she joined Hannah and Peter. As she worked, her mind drifted back to her childhood, to the afternoons she'd spent with her grandmother.

She could practically smell the scent of freshly cut grass, the sunshine on her shoulders as she bicycled the few blocks to Nan's house. Like so many times when her older sisters would skip off to hang out with their friends, Sharon would while away the afternoon at her grandmother's house, doing a puzzle together or helping her bake something.

Her grandmother had been the first to notice what she referred to as the 'gift'. For Sharon it had always been more like a curse. She'd told her not to fear it, that it was just another sense like hearing or seeing, except that not everyone had it.

"Some people are gifted athletes, Sharon," Nana said. "Others are gifted musicians, and other people just have a special knack with math, right? Well, people like you and me... we just have a gift that most other people don't even believe exists."

Nan had the gift as well, but not as strong as Sharon's. She'd be able to tell if a storm was coming or if an old friend or relative was about to ring her on the telephone. Sharon had the same ability; it was a game they'd play together, giving each other a knowing wink when it turned out they had predicted correctly.

But Sharon's gift had made her seem odd to other children. She could find lost items easily and often knew secrets about her classmates that no one else knew. Before it got too out of hand, Nan advised her to keep her own counsel about those kinds of things.

"People fear what they don't understand, Sharon. And children can be very, very cruel. You don't want your friends to be afraid of you, do you?"

But the one instance that always stuck out in her memory was the day she and Nan walked to the store together to pick up some items for a bake sale. They had to go by a deserted old house that Sharon always avoided when she was out riding her bike in the neighborhood. But it wasn't just Sharon, most kids were wary of it, so that wasn't all that unique. Nan had stopped right in front of it, staring up at the second-floor windows. She'd held Sharon's hand and her voice was soft when she asked, "Tell me what you see, Shar."

Sharon could easily recall the dizzy nausea that rumbled in her gut that day along with that electrical sensation up her spine to her head as she clung to her grandmother, watching the house. In her mind's eye she watched a burly man, crazed with drink strangle his family in their sleep before hanging himself. "I don't want to look, Nan. It's bad. Bad, bad things happened there!"

Her grandmother had agreed. "Yes, I know the story. It happened many years ago. Tell me what you feel standing here."

Tears had sprung into Sharon's eyes as she tugged on her Nan's hand, trying to leave. "He hurt them. His own kids. I can't think of it, Nan! Don't make me!"

Her grandmother had nodded and hugged her close as they'd walked away. "I know, sweetie. I'm sorry, I was curious." But Sharon still could see the scene in her mind, even to this day. It haunted her. That scenario from the past played a role in why she had chosen to work in schools helping children.

She paused for a moment, wondering about the way her

43

mind had drifted off to memories she hadn't thought of in years and years. They had all started coming back to her when she'd felt that touch on her face and the sensation of being watched in the family room. This house had rekindled not only the memories, but the physical feelings also returned. And she hadn't had those since childhood.

Sharon stood up and brushed the loose dirt from her hands. This 'gift' and Liam's presence in her home wasn't something she wanted to experience. She went back into the house, casting a pointed glance at the staircase as she walked by the dining room. If she could figure out a way to get this ghost to move on, that might mean that she would never have any weird dreams or that awful feeling again. As she scrubbed her hands in the bathroom sink, watching the dirty water drain she sighed. If only getting this ghost or spirit to leave were as easy as this.

When the screen door banged shut from the sunroom, she jumped.

Hannah's voice drifted from the family room, "We're done in the yard, Mom. I'm going for my run now."

"Okay. Have fun." It was a surprise even to her own ears in how normal she sounded. When she heard Hannah's feet thumping down the steps again leading to the yard, she breathed a sigh of relief. If the girl knew what had happened in the office, she'd be seriously scared. For the first time, Sharon was happy that Hannah was staying in the city, working in the bakery... at least until she figured out what to do about this ghost.

There had to be some way of getting Liam to leave them in peace.

EIGHT

While hannah was out for her afternoon run, Sharon and Peter sorted through the papers in the office, placing them in the file cabinet.

When he'd first seen the box overturned and the heap of papers, he'd been stunned. But gradually that shock was replaced with anger. He reread the letter that had been left for them and looked at her, "This is crazy. Frankly, I'm more than a little T'd off that the previous owners never said a thing about this. They must have experienced some odd stuff. Maybe that was why they sold it, not because of a divorce."

Sharon filed the last of the papers and then turned to him. "If we'd known, would we have still bought this place? I'm not sure it would have stopped us. I mean, we both fell in love with the house. It's perfect for what we need. If this is the worst we have to deal with, we can manage, although I'm not crazy about anything fiddling with electricity. That's too scary."

Peter edged the office chair closer to the desk and clicked the laptop, watching the screensaver change to the familiar Google search home page. "I'll see if there's anything online about Liam Gallagher in Westport. Sometimes there are archives of old newspapers online." He typed in the search bar and waited for the results to populate.

When the page loaded, he did an eye-roll, "Great. Just our luck there would be a rock star with that same name flooding the internet."

"I might make out better in the archives at the local library. Why not try asking how best to deal with a ghost in your home? There's got to be something we can do." Placing her hand on his shoulder, she bent slightly to see the screen. When the screen populated with this latest query, she pointed at the third one down. "That one. Open it."

The title was *What To Do If Your House Is Haunted, A 'How-To' Guide'*.

She skimmed the page that loaded, whispering aloud the key points, "... have a healthy skepticism ... keep a journal of what happens, the time, date and the weather outside."

"I wonder why the weather?" Peter glanced up at her.

"Maybe it has something to do with the static electricity in the air, like before a storm or the cycle of the moon." She continued skimming ahead, *"... once you've ruled out logical explanations like a window open or electrical issues, or even rodents, you can accept the novelty of a ghost in your home or you can enlist the help of a ghost researcher."*

"A ghostbuster is what they mean." Peter clicked the mouse and closed the lid of the laptop. "We're not calling any ghostbusters in. The next thing you know, we'll be the star of some ghost hunter show. It's all so ridiculous."

Sharon examined Peter's face when he turned to her. Was he downplaying all this for her benefit or his own? He was probably more unsettled by this than he was letting on.

She nodded, "I agree we're not there... yet. We'll try keeping a journal and get an electrician in to examine the wiring." She looked at the windows framing the office nook. Although they were open, there hadn't been a breeze that day capable of lifting any boxes. It was a late summer, blue-sky kind of day. Who was she trying to kid? It would have had to have been one hell of a storm to have tossed those boxes and papers around. And leaving that note arranged on top? No, it was Liam's handiwork.

Peter let out a huff of air. "We should start dinner. Hannah will be back from her run soon." He got up and paused before walking out of the room, "You coming?"

She sat down in the chair, already reaching to get the laptop up and running again. "I'll start that journal and maybe do a little more research. I'll be down soon. The steaks are defrosting in the fridge for the barbecue. I'll get the salad ready if you start the other stuff."

"Okay. Don't be too long. I know what kind of time vampire the internet can be." With that, he left the room.

Sharon continued reading articles from her online search, looking for ones that appeared credible. As if online articles could be credible… But then, the New York Times had a piece on dealing with ghosts. The main take-away that resonated with her was that they weren't exactly powerless in dealing with a spirit lingering in their house. One approach, which many people who'd dealt with this advised, was to respectfully ask the entity to stop.

She smiled reading that. This was something she could do. In fact, how many times when she'd counseled a kid being bullied had she advised the child to do just that—state your case and ask the bully to stop. She'd try that, and if that didn't work, they could then bump the problem up for a higher authority to assist. In this case, a higher authority would mean getting a ghost hunter or medium to help.

When she stood up and closed the laptop, she took a deep breath looking around the bedroom. In a low but steady voice, she spoke, "Liam Gallagher, if you're here, you need to leave my stuff alone. No turning on the TV, locking me in a room or upsetting my office. You leave Hannah, Peter and any guests that come here, alone."

Only silence answered her command. She could feel her face grow warm from mild embarrassment as her gaze flitted around the room. It was strange doing this. Speaking out loud to a ghost? Even as a child she'd never communicated with the dead, just sensed their presence. But if it worked, then it was worth it.

She walked across the room and came to a halt in the doorway. She inhaled sharply a few times, sniffing the air. There was a faint aroma of sweet smoke, like pipe tobacco. She gripped the doorframe when a spell of vertigo washed through her. Her eyes opened wider. Oh, my God. That smell was Liam's answer. And the feeling, the dizziness and the hair on her arms tingling confirmed that he was there. She'd got through to him and he was acknowledging it with that odor of pipe tobacco.

She took a few deep calming breaths before leaving the doorway and going down the stairs to join her husband. It was probably too soon to know for sure if she'd been successful, but the smell of that smoke helped to ease her mind.

She could handle this.

The smell of sautéed onions infused the air in the kitchen where Peter stood scrubbing potatoes. He turned from the sink, hearing her approach. "Well? Anything new to report? Hannah's outside looking after the steaks."

"I read a couple more articles on dealing with this. It's amazing how many there are." She joined him at the sink. "I spoke to him, the ghost. I asked him to leave the electricity and my stuff, alone."

"What about my stuff?"

"Okay, *our* stuff. "She got the lettuce out of the fridge and rinsed it, glancing over at Peter. "You know, I think I may have gotten through to him. There was a faint odor of pipe tobacco just before I left the bedroom. That's the first time I smelled that in this house."

"Great. An unwelcome ghost who smokes. It just keeps getting better and better." He smiled to let her know he was teasing. "I have to admit, you seem much calmer about this."

She nodded. "I am. I'll still do all the other things—the research, the journal and calling an electrician. Asking him to respect our boundaries and leave us in peace also seems like the right thing to do." She glanced at the doorway when

Hannah stepped inside.

"I ran out of BBQ sauce. We have more, right?" Hannah walked to the fridge to check.

"Of course. There's an unopened one in the pantry." Sharon dried her hands and went over to get it. "Here you go." Handing it to her daughter, she continued, "We'll eat in the dining room tonight. It's our first proper dinner in our new home, so we should christen it."

"Sure. That sounds good." She paused in the doorway and turned to her mother, "The hot tub is barely seventy degrees. I'm not sure it'll be ready this evening."

Peter gave Sharon a quick glance before answering for both of them, "I vote we forgo the hot tub and just go for a walk after dinner. Maybe get an ice cream cone. What do you say?"

She felt her chest loosen at his words. Until they had an electrician in, or were sure they could control this entity in their home, the thought of going into a hot tub was anything but relaxing. "Okay. I'd like that. It'll give us a chance to explore the neighborhood a bit."

Peter got the plates and cutlery out and carried on setting the dining room table while she finished with the salad.

All the while she worked chopping vegetables, it felt like someone was watching her every move. A couple of times her gaze flitted over to the doorway leading to the other room. Even though nothing was visible there, she felt a presence.

And tomorrow she'd be all alone in the house.

NINE

Later that evening, on their way home from strolling around the neighborhood and small main street, they came to the house at the lakeside which was being renovated. Sharon glanced up, taking in the detailed gingerbread molding clinging to the eaves two-and-a-half stories above them. French doors led to a small balcony on the second floor, where the trim work continued.

There was a man and woman in their twenties working in the front yard of the stately house. For a couple so young, having such a beautiful home on the lake was a little unusual to Sharon. They were just a few years older than Hannah and living in such a lovely house.

The woman looked up from where she was raking and smiled seeing them walking by the low wooden fence. "Hi. Nice evening for a walk." She dropped the rake and extended her hand, hurrying over. "I'm Sandy Pratt."

With a firm grip, she shook Sharon's hand. Sharon couldn't help but smile back at the friendliness in Sandy's eyes that accompanied her smile. "I'm Sharon Phelps and this is my husband Peter and our daughter, Hannah."

She watched the younger woman shake hands with her family while from the edge of her vision she could see Sandy's husband wander over.

Sandy grabbed his wrist, pulling him closer, "This is my husband, James." He was the opposite in complexion to Sandy's olive tone. He was pale with military cut, blonde hair and he was at least a head taller than his wife. From his trim and fit physique, James looked like he was no stranger to the gym.

Sharon extended her hand, "Please to meet you, James. I'm Sharon." She watched as both Peter and Hannah introduced themselves. While Sandy bubbled with friendliness James was much more reserved, his lips trying, but not managing a smile.

Even though James seemed wary, Sandy looked like she'd be fun to hang out with. Sharon remarked, "Your home is beautiful. I see you're doing renovations with all the workers and vans coming and going."

Sandy's mouth fell open, and she blurted, "Oh Gosh! I hope they didn't wake you too early in the morning!"

When Sharon shook her head, Sandy continued, "The house has been in James's family forever, although it's been vacant for the last ten years. We left Toronto to restore it to its former glory. We've had enough of big city life. It was time for a change."

Hannah chimed in, "I'm the opposite. I can't wait to finish school and live in a big city."

"You'll change your tune once you've been there a few years. When you're not looking over your shoulder because of the gang violence, it feels like you're living in a United Nations refugee camp!" James snorted, throwing shade on Hannah's enthusiasm.

Sandy interjected, smiling up at her husband. "It wasn't all bad. Some of the guys you played hockey with were nice." She practically beamed when she looked over at Sharon and Peter. "The Leaf's scouted James when he was in college. He just about made the cut to be signed on with the team."

Peter's eyes lit up, as Sharon knew they would. While the

Toronto Maple Leafs weren't his favourite team, he was a die-hard hockey fan. He looked at James and grinned, "Wow! We're neighbors with someone who tried out for a major league team? That's impressive."

But instead of relishing Peter's compliment, James dismissed it. "*Almost* only counts when you're playing horse-shoes. Besides, all that's in the past. It doesn't matter now."

If Sharon hadn't been watching James's face closely, she would have missed the fleeting scowl he shot at his wife. She glanced at Sandy and saw her cheeks flush at his silent censure.

She changed the subject, pointing down and across the street where their butter-yellow, two-story home sat. "That's our place. We just moved in the other day!" She couldn't help but smile with pride when she added, "I'm planning on opening a B&B there. Peter works in a town nearby." She rubbed her daughter's arm affectionately, "Hannah has left the nest. She's here visiting from Kingston."

"Are you in college or university, now?" Sandy's gaze fastened on Hannah.

"University next year. Right now, I'm working in a bakery trying to save money for school."

Peter directed his comment to James, "So your family lived in Westport? And you're restoring the old homestead? It's a beautiful spot, right on the lake. I don't blame you for coming here to live."

James looked down at the ground, before he answered, "Yeah, but I actually never lived here. My cousin tried making a go of the house but he almost went bankrupt and had to give it up, from what I understand." He rolled his eyes and looked at Sandy, "The renovations are going painfully slow. I've tried to help the guys get things moving along faster, but that hasn't worked out well."

Sandy swatted his arm playfully, "I really wish you wouldn't. Every time you pick up a hammer or saw you end up hurting yourself." She smiled at Sharon, "Honestly, I've gone through a box of Band-Aids."

"Oh no." Sharon noticed James's face flush red and the

muscle in his jaw tighten. This was obviously a sore point between the couple, in more ways than one. She glanced up at Peter before edging away. "It was really nice to meet you. We're keeping you from your yard work and the light is getting low. We'd better get going."

Peter shook James' hands and murmured, "Take it easy. Try not to kill yourself with the renos. It's a beautiful house."

With that, they waved and continued on their way home.

When they were out of earshot, Sharon commented, "She's nice but he's kind of distant. I don't think he appreciated us stopping. I can't imagine him even wanting to be on a big sports team. He doesn't seem the type."

"Maybe he's shy. He could be bitter he didn't make the team and doesn't like talking about it. Who knows?" Peter pulled Sharon closer and kissed her temple, "Not everyone is as lucky as you to snag a charmer like me."

"Who's the modest one now, Dad?" Hannah looked over at her mother, "Yeah, Sandy's friendly but James… well, his eyes were flat, kind of dead looking to me."

Peter muttered while his gaze focused on the house across the street from their own. "Speaking of dead… That old lady is out on her verandah again." He raised his hand and waved to her.

When Sharon looked the old woman stared straight at them but never acknowledged the greeting. She'd been there the day before when they'd moved into the house but hadn't even given so much as a nod. "Maybe she has poor vision. Older people often have cataracts."

Hannah glanced over at the woman. "She's like that old guy in the attic, in that movie, *The Sentinel*. I'm not sure I like our neighbors. I can't wait to live in a big city, despite what James Pratt said. I think he's a racist."

"Yeah, that remark about living in the United Nations. I thought that was inappropriate." Sharon forced a smile. "But that's just two people. I'm sure there are lots of friendly folks in this town."

They opened the gate and walked across the deck to get to

the set of stairs. Sharon admired the solar lights Peter and Hannah had placed around the small pond when she got to the top step. The murmur of trickling water below was the only sound in the cool air, a chilly reminder that autumn was just around the corner.

When they stepped inside the family room, a wave of heat hit Sharon's face. The room was like a sauna even though the window overlooking the yard below was open!

Peter rushed to the thermostat to check the setting. But even as he went there, the click-click sound of the electrical heating units at the baseboards powering up again, sounded.

"What's with the heat?" Hannah stared at her mother and then her father. "You never turn the heat on until it's practically the first snowfall!"

Peter turned the setting of the thermostat to 'off' and scowled when he turned to Sharon. "I didn't turn that on. Did you?"

"I'd better check my room. There's no way I can sleep in this hothouse." Hannah raced up the stairs.

When Hannah was out of earshot, Sharon hissed, "I think we both know how that heat setting got turned up." She watched Peter shake his head and storm out of the room to the kitchen and the rest of the rooms.

Her eyes narrowed when she looked around the room, "Liam. I told you to stop messing with the electricity. Don't do that again!"

She wedged the door open to let the suffocating heat out to the screened-in sunroom. Fanning herself with her hand, she strode up the set of stairs leading to the guest room where Hannah was.

Hannah turned from where she'd lifted the window high. "Mom, this is seriously creepy. I know that you and Dad didn't turn the heat on. Plus, no animal got in and draped toilet paper everywhere. And then there was getting locked in the basement. This place is haunted, Mom."

Sharon sighed, closing her eyes to hide the fact that she agreed with her daughter. But she also didn't want to frighten

Hannah more than she already was. She stepped over to her daughter, "I agree that there are odd things happening here. But before we jump to the conclusion that there's some kind of ghost screwing with our house, we need to rule out logical explanations. Your father and I will book an electrician to inspect the wiring, especially now that the heat just came on like that."

"Wasn't that part of the home inspection? Is it safe to even *be* here?" Hannah shook her head slowly and her eyes narrowed. "There's more going on here than you're letting on, Mom."

Sharon could feel her cheeks grow warm from being caught out in a lie. "I think we have to take this one step at a time. The logical explanation is some kind of short or power surge. We'll leave that to the experts."

From the look on her daughter's face, Sharon could tell that she wasn't buying 'the logical' explanation. Her next words confirmed it. "Why did the previous owners leave a house full of antiques? It kind of seems like they just wanted out—fast. There's something strange going on here, Mom, and you know it."

Sharon's fingers grazed Hannah's ear when she lifted a stray lock of her daughter's hair and tucked it into place. "If it will make you more comfortable, why don't you sleep in the room next to ours? Or at least leave the door between the two sections of the house open tonight?"

"No. I like my room. I've got my own bathroom and I have things the way I like it." Hannah's jaw clenched tight before she added, "This house is haunted, Mom. That's what I think. And if that's the case… well, I will not be driven out of my room. I'll leave the connecting door open, but that's as far as I'm willing to concede."

Sharon smiled, watching the fire in Hannah's eyes. Peter was right about one thing. Her daughter was strong, becoming more like her every day.

"Okay. Let's go downstairs and see how your father's making out. He's probably having a conniption, seeing dollars streaming out the windows from all this." She placed an arm around Hannah and steered her to the stairs.

So much for reasoning with this entity. There had to be something else that would work. If this kept up, there was no way they could carry on living there, let alone have paying guests.

TEN

The next morning, after seeing Peter and Hannah off, the quiet in the house weighed down on Sharon. Hugging her arms tight to her body, she wandered into the kitchen to tidy up the breakfast things. All the while she rinsed the plates and stacked them in the dishwasher her movements felt jerky. When a knife slipped from her hand, clattering onto the floor she jumped back.

Closing her eyes for a few moments, she gripped the edge of the countertop and counted to ten. Taking deep breaths, she settled her nerves enough that she could pick up the knife.

This was ridiculous. She shouldn't feel on edge, waiting for something weird to happen. It was *her* home, dammit. She had things arranged the way she liked them and no ghost, this Liam character, would spoil it for her.

She turned her cell phone on to the music app and plugged it into the small speaker. When Bruce Springsteen started playing, she focused on the beat in her steps walking back and forth from the table to the fridge putting things away.

When she was done, she picked up the phone and did a search for electrical companies in the area. When the first couple calls went to voicemail right away, she ended up leaving a request for a callback.

With the phone in hand, she left the kitchen to go upstairs to her bedroom. Even though she'd decided to delay booking guests until they had this under control, there was nothing stopping her from working on the website for the B&B. That would take some time to get up and running, anyway.

She settled in at the desk in her office nook to begin work. More than a few times she paused reading the on-line 'how to's' and glanced over her shoulder at the space behind her.

It was funny. She was still jittery, although she didn't feel a presence watching her work like she'd felt in the kitchen the day before. That the ghost was gone was probably too much to hope for at this stage.

Almost three hours later, she rose from the office chair and stretched her neck muscles. She glanced at the webpage she'd created. It was almost complete, but she wasn't sure about the layout. When her stomach rumbled with hunger, she decided that a break was definitely in order.

She went downstairs and plugged her phone into the tiny speaker once more while she made some lunch. The music halted when the ding of a text message sounded from her phone. She smiled seeing the message was from Hannah, back at her place in the city after the weekend.

> **How is everything going, Mom? All quiet there? Anything else weird happening? BTW, I got the weekend off so I'll be out to see you and Dad.**

Sharon's fingers flew, typing an answer.

> **Everything's fine! I'm so glad you will be home this weekend! I'd like you to take a look at my webpage. I think it needs something, but I'm not sure what.**

The response was immediate.

> **K. Gotta go now. Customers coming in. TTYL**

Sharon smiled and clicked the music icon again. She walked to the fridge to grab a soft drink.

Suddenly, the music blared!

She jerked back, almost dropping the can of soda. What the hell? The noise resounded through the room, even vibrating in her stomach. Rushing to the table, she clicked the icon to shut it down. When silence descended her racing pulse pounded in her ears.

Peering around the room, she gripped the edge of the table to steady herself. She willed her breathing to slow down, trying to calm herself. Her voice was a hiss when she whispered, "Liam, I told you to leave my things alone. This isn't funny!"

Gritting her teeth, she slipped her phone into the pocket of her hoodie, and took her sandwich and soda into the sunroom. She gazed out at her yard, while her mind spun with what had just happened. Again, Liam had startled her with his stupid prank. What was worse was the fact that he'd been in the room with her and she hadn't sensed it. Somehow he was getting better at concealing himself until the last minute. This had to stop.

The library. She'd finish her lunch and then go there. Having seen it on their walk last night, it was about six blocks away; it would be faster to take the car. Plus, she needed to pick up a few things at the grocery store, anyway.

She chewed her sandwich and washed it down with a long swallow of soda. Damn it! This shouldn't be happening. She should finish her web page, but instead of that she had to go research this Liam character to see how to get him to leave them in peace.

Maybe he had a wife or kids in the afterlife that they could convince him to go to. He definitely had a child—whoever the author of that note she found with the legal papers was. And that child had probably passed away too; the family had bought the place almost a hundred years ago. He'd be more welcome in Heaven than he was here, scaring the daylights out of everyone.

She returned to the kitchen and put the lunch fixings away.

After finger combing her shoulder length hair up into a loose knot, she stepped over to the doorway to grab the key to her Honda. Her mouth popped open seeing the row of empty cup hooks under the small whiteboard.

Her keys! She always hung them up when she came in the house. It was her motto—a place for everything and everything in its place.

Had Peter or Hannah moved them? She shook her head. No. They'd never do that. She went to the family room where she'd left her purse on the off chance it was there. Maybe with all that had happened, she'd slipped up and left them there. She rummaged for a bit and then tipped it upside down, spilling the contents onto the sofa. Still no keys, just her wallet, lipstick, a checkbook and some coins.

But she hadn't used the car since the day they'd moved in, two days ago. She went from room to room lifting pillows, checking counters, coffee tables and even the rain coat hanging next to the front door.

"Damn it! Where are my keys!" She stomped up the stairs and rifled through the two bedside tables, her desk and filing cabinet drawer. Nothing.

Opening the adjoining bathroom, she peered at the counter. But only a jar of face cream and Peter's shaving cream sat there. As she was turning to leave, her gaze hitched to the white porcelain bathtub. Her key ring key rested close to the drain.

She bent, snatching the key into her fist. There was no way that anyone—A LIVING PERSON, THAT IS—would put her keys there. That left one culprit.

She scowled, looking around the room. 'LIAM! YOU ARE HISTORY!'"

ELEVEN

The library, with its steeply peaked metal roof over a limestone building, was wedged in between a modern post office and a stately home. Judging by the stained glass windows and the wide set of stone steps, it was probably a church from the last century which the community had outgrown.

When she entered the building, a woman in her fifties with glasses perched near the end of her nose looked up from the computer set before her. Deep lines framed the smile that creased a longish face, and her dark eyes crinkled at the corners. "Hello."

Sharon walked over to the desk. "Hi. I wonder if you have old copies of Westport's newspapers from the 1940's to the 1950's? I am looking for information on a person who once lived in the house we bought."

The smile fell from the older woman's face as she slowly rose, "I wish I could help you with that. Unfortunately, the newspaper you're referring to, *The Mirror*, was purchased thirty years ago. The new guy running the paper destroyed all the old copies before the library could get them."

Sharon felt her stomach sink. She'd counted on those newspaper records being available. "Why would he do that?

That was local history."

The woman shook her head before she extended her hand, "I'm Lillian Babcock. I agree. It was such a stupid, short-sighted thing to do."

"I'm Sharon Phelps."

"Welcome to Westport." Lillian's eyes narrowed in thought, "I might be able to help you, despite the missing newspapers. A volunteer in the community has compiled binders of obituary notices. There might be something about...what name did you say you're looking for?"

"Liam Gallagher." Sharon pulled out the letter and the land title document from her purse and handed it to Lillian. She watched the other woman's eyebrows arch as she read the letter. "Odd little note, right?"

"Suspected foul play. That would have made the newspaper. Too bad the jackass destroyed them." Lillian handed the papers back and added, "The binders are downstairs. I'll bring them up and I'll help you search through them."

"Really? That's nice for you to offer to help but—"

"Are you kidding? I am bored out of my mind sitting here. The only thing you interrupted was a game of Free Cell on the computer. I'd welcome a diversion. I only work here part time to give my aunt and me a break from each other. I'm kind of new to Westport as well." She snorted a laugh, "Been here five years, but I'm still an outsider."

Sharon smiled, "I guess my husband and I are in that category." She watched Lillian walk to the back of the library and disappear through a door. An obituary, if she could find one on Liam, might corroborate or disprove the letter she'd found. It might also list any relatives who survived him.

Sharon wandered around the room where racks of books lined the walls. The place had a quaint feel in the handwritten labels denoting the genres. After a few minutes Lillian appeared in the doorway at the back with two huge black binders in her arms. They were a lot thicker than Sharon would have thought. It was a good thing Lillian had offered to help.

"I don't get many people here, especially not on a weekday." Lillian set the binders on a long table which was nestled near a window overlooking the street outside.

Sharon took a seat across from Lillian and opened the binder before her. Yellowed newspaper clippings of deaths over the years, along with marriages and births were pasted onto the ivory pages.

"You said 1940's?" Lillian looked over and adjusted her eyeglasses higher on her nose.

"Yes. Liam and his wife Ginny took possession of the house —it's 23 Maple by the way —in 1940. The next record shows the house being sold through an Executor, in 1951." Sharon gazed at the clippings, which were all in the 1980's. They arranged the book with more recent dates at the front, which made sense.

"My aunt Mary might remember some of this. Maybe not directly, but she could have heard stories passed down. If this man was drowned on purpose, it had to have caused a stir. Have you considered trying police records? It would have been the Provincials who investigated if they suspected foul play." Lillian peered over at Sharon for a few moments.

"True. But I thought I'd start here. Police records—if I can get access to them—will be my next resource." She skimmed through the bolder headlines on that page, but she was still only in the 1960's.

"This is an interesting exercise, especially after seeing that letter. Many people might not go to the trouble of finding out more. You must be kind of a history buff to want to do this." Lillian examined Sharon's face.

Sharon knew Lillian was fishing, and she deliberated for a few moments on whether to tell her of the strange goings on in her home. The older woman was so sensible and down to earth that she might think Sharon was some kind of nutcase. On the other hand, Lillian had offered to help. She could at least be honest with her.

"No, in a past life I was a social worker. My house, the one we bought, is kind of... different. Some odd things have happened since we moved in a few days ago. I'm trying to find answers." Now it was her turn to inspect Lillian's reaction.

"Odd, you say? You mean, spooky type things? You suspect that this guy might be haunting your house?" Lillian would be a talented poker player in how unreadable her features were.

"I know it sounds crazy." Sharon described all the things that had happened.

Lillian's mouth fell open wider and wider as she listened. So much for having a poker face. Finally, she spoke. "You poor thing! The stress of a move and then encountering this kind of weird stuff. 23 Maple... Is your place the bright yellow one on the corner?"

Sharon gaped at her for a few beats. Was the haunting in her house public knowledge? "Yes! What do you know about it?"

Lillian pulled back. "Nothing. I've walked by it. I chatted with the couple who lived there before you. They broke up, I hear. I honestly know nothing about your house."

Lillian seemed sincere. Sharon breathed a sigh of relief and went back to scanning the binder. But still something niggled at the back of her mind. "Please don't mention this to anyone. I'm trying to set up a B&B and I don't need this kind of talk going round."

Lillian leaned forward, "Trust me, I won't say a word. But I will ask my aunt Mary about Liam Gallagher. She knows a lot of people in this village and the history."

Sharon looked over at Lillian, "Do you believe in this kind of thing? Ghosts and hauntings?" Lillian seemed like a no-nonsense type of person. She looked down at the book again. Why did she care what Lillian thought? Except that she did.

Lillian's gaze softened, and she plucked her glasses off. "I discount nothing anymore. There have been too many things I've read about that can be explained by a purely scientific point of view." She laughed, "That doesn't mean I'm going to join that gang of people storming area 51. Although I believe the government knows more about aliens than they're letting on." She wiped her glasses on her sweater and then put them on again. "I believe you, Sharon. That's all I'm saying. Something is not right in your home and you want it to stop, right?"

"Thank you. I don't really know you, but I appreciate you saying that—not to mention all the help going through these books." Sharon made a mental note to bring cookies in when she visited the library the next time.

"No need to thank me. I'm a public servant without a public." Lillian laughed at her own joke and resumed reading.

For the next forty minutes the two women scoured the binders looking for any mention of Liam Gallagher.

Finally, Sharon closed the binder, no wiser than when she entered the library. Some items had been interesting, in a quirky, historical kind of way, but that was it.

Lillian rose and went to the desk to get her phone. "Let me have your cell number, Sharon. If I find out anything from Aunt Mary, I'll call you."

Sharon followed her over to the desk and pulled her own cell phone out. After they exchanged numbers, Lillian looked aside, her fingers tapping on the desk while she thought. "Another path you could try is genealogical societies in Brockville. They cover our area as well as their own. And cemeteries. There might be something on-line that you could access."

"Yeah. I never thought of that. Liam may even be buried in that cemetery on the outskirts of town—next to his wife." Sharon didn't have time to do that today, but maybe tomorrow. "It was nice meeting you, Lillian! Thanks for all your help."

"Any time! See you later."

Sharon glanced at the sky as she walked down the granite steps. An inky dark cloud above threatened to let loose a torrential downpour sometime soon. She hurried down the street where she had parked the car. A quick check on the dash showed that it was almost four o'clock. Peter would be home in two hours. She had plenty of time to get to the grocery store and get supper on before he arrived.

The route to the grocery store took her past the Pratt home where a white van with a blue logo denoting Mahone Electric was parked. On impulse, she pulled in and got out. Maybe the electrician working there would pop by her home to check for problems. It might be faster than waiting for a call-back from the outfits she'd contacted.

As she was about to knock on the front door to the home, when it was thrown open. Sandy and James Pratt jerked back upon seeing her. There was a towel around James' hand that was stained with a blotch of red. From the pained look in his eyes, it was clear he was injured. "Oh my God, what happened?"

Sandy spoke before James had a chance to. "He was working on the dock and sliced his hand. We're heading to the clinic now, to get it stitched up."

James clutched the towel with his other hand, adjusting the pressure. "We can't talk now; we've got to go."

"No. No. No. Go on! Get to the doctor." Sharon stepped back, allowing them to pass by. She followed them, and opened the door to her car. Somehow with them gone, it didn't seem right to enter the home to speak to the electrician. She'd just have to wait for the other ones she'd called to get back to her.

She backed out and through the rear-view mirror she saw the Pratts hightail it up the street in the opposite direction. From the looks of it, she wasn't the only one having a hard time adjusting to a new home. She had a ghost but James was in over his head trying to help with the construction. He should leave it to the professionals and call it a day.

As she drove along the waterfront she glanced at the lake, wondering where Liam had drowned? For all she knew it could at the small marina or even near the bridge. There was no sign of a fountain that the letter had mentioned.

Damn that foolish newspaper guy for destroying answers to that question!

TWELVE

The next day Peter worked from home applying the finishing touches to the company's third-quarter financial statement. He could focus better at home, to complete it before the teleconference meeting that afternoon. Plus, he'd be here for Sharon if she needed him. The previous day had been more than a little unsettling for her.

As he worked at the dining room table with files spread out before him, he glanced around the room. The house was quiet as a tomb. Even the night before had been normal in every respect, although they'd both been on edge waiting for their resident ghost's next caper.

It was just after noon when Sharon popped in from the kitchen where she'd been baking biscuits to freeze. "Would you like some lunch? I reheated left-over's from dinner."

Peter clicked the laptop to close the spreadsheet and looked over at her. The rosy flush on her face from baking and the twinkle in her blue eyes made her look like she was in her twenties, not a hint of closing in on fifty. And her movements still held that smooth athletic quality, a result of many marathon runs.

He stood up, "Sure! I'd better make it quick though. I still have a few tweaks on this report before I send it off to the others."

She finished wiping her hands on the tea towel onto her shoulder, "That meeting is at two, right? I'll do some errands while your meeting is happening to stay out of your hair. I made cookies that I'd like to take to Lillian at the library and then I need to get fresh fruit at the store."

He inhaled deeply, following her into the kitchen. The smell of fresh baking, as usual, lifted his spirits while making his mouth water. "I hope you aren't taking all the cookies to your new friend."

She rolled her eyes before getting the lasagna from the oven. When his hand shot past her to snatch a cookie, she gave him a soft hip-check. "You and your sweet tooth. That plate is for you, of course. I already filled a bag for Lillian."

When her cell phone rang, he watched her grab it and then mouth "Electrician'. Well, that was one item they would be able to check off. But maybe things would quiet down of their own accord if the previous night and morning were any sign.

He took a couple of plates from the cabinet and dished out the lasagna as Sharon set up a time for the electrician to come out. After a few minutes, she joined him at the table.

"He'll be here tomorrow morning. I might pop by the Pratt's house before I come home to see how James is."

He continued eating and then looked over at her, "Yeah. Had to have been bad to get stitches."

Sharon was quiet for a few beats as she ate, but from the faraway look in her eyes it was clear she was thinking. "There's a Liam Gallagher in the cemetery on the outskirts of town. I did a web search this morning and found it. It's got to be him. There was no record of Ginny, his wife, but maybe Ginny was her middle name. I might pop in there to see if I can find his grave."

"You've got a packed afternoon. Why don't you hold off on visiting the cemetery, and I'll go with you after the meeting? I should be finished by four."

"Okay. It'll be good for you to get out into the fresh air. We'll go together."

***

Later that afternoon, Peter sat in the family room with the laptop hooked into the TV monitor. He had printed the agenda and set it next to him, before clicking the icon to join the webinar. The screen populated with Amy, his assistant and his boss Alf Lane sitting across from the two directors from Product Development and Marketing. They looked up from their notes when Peter's face appeared on the monitor at the end of the conference room.

"Hi Peter." It was Amy who piped up, setting the volume before leaving the room.

Alf Lane began speaking, outlining the agenda topics and reports they would be discussing.

BANG!

Peter stiffened at the loud crash coming from the floor above. It had sounded like a door slamming shut. Alf stopped talking and looked at the monitor. All eyes focused on Peter.

"I'm sorry. The wind must have caught an open door in my house. Please carry on." Although Peter's voice was calm, his pulse rate had jumped to hypersonic levels. Oh, my God. He'd checked the bedroom that morning to ensure that nothing had fiddled with the electrical baseboard heating unit. He was certain he'd closed the door up there.

"If you're sure, Peter?" The smirk on Josh Clarke's yap made Peter's face grow warm. Trust him to try to undercut everyone and anyone to make himself look good.

Alf turned back to the screen, which had split into two sides. A bar chart showed the changes in production over the last three quarters. At this point, the director of product development started speaking.

Footsteps overhead caught Peter's attention for a moment and his hand shot to the sound icon to 'mute' the audio input from his microphone. Shit! It had to be Liam! Just when it looked like the coast was clear, he'd shown up to mess with him and this meeting!

The footsteps continued slowly, each thud plucking the nerves in Peter's neck. The creak of a floorboard sent a shiver through Peter's shoulders. His gaze darted to the staircase where he half expected the steps to continue. Oh crap.

He turned back to the monitor, saying a silent prayer that the activity in his house would stop. On his screen, all eyes were now on him. Oh man...

"Peter? Do you have anything to add to Richard's graph?"

He clicked the button to un-mute his mic. "No." Assessing the brief glimpse of the chart he'd seen on the last slide, his mind raced. "It seems quite in order with what you'll find in my report. All on the upswing. Please continue."

Alf gave him a puzzled look before nodding to the Director of Product Development. Peter wasted no time in muting once more. Yeah, his answer had been anything but original or informative.

A trickle of sweat ran down the side of his face as he sat watching the monitor, half listening to the meeting. He perched on the edge of the sofa, his knee twitching up and down, expecting... What the hell would happen next?

He didn't have long to wait. The timer on the microwave beeped and continued beeping. 'Stairway to Heaven' started blaring from the sound system on the other side of the house. Peter's breath caught in his throat, barely breathing as he carried on, pretending to be part of the meeting.

Thank God, they couldn't hear what was going on in his home at that minute. But eventually he'd be forced to un-mute to comment and the cacophony would blast in the background. Once more, they directed a question at him.

He could feel his neck muscles grow tight as his mind raced. He made a gesture as if he was clicking to un-mute the sound and scowled at it. Throwing his hands in the air before him, he shook his head and then grabbed a pen and paper.

Technical problems. Sorry, I can't communicate with you. Carry on. I'm listening.' He held the paper up, aiming it at the camera lens in the laptop.

Alf did a theatrical eye roll before turning back to the

others at the table.

Peter's stomach settled lower, and he breathed a sigh of relief. His reputation of having awful luck with electronic equipment was kind of a joke at work. Hopefully, that would buy him a pass this time.

There was no way he wanted to un-mute and let them hear the chaos happening in his home. Who would believe he wasn't having some kind of party on company time—which in the scheme of things might be more plausible than trying to explain that his home was haunted.

He grabbed his cell phone and typed a text message to his assistant, Amy.

> 'Go back into the meeting and cover for me. I'm having technical issues on my end. I can see and hear but my audio input is down.'

After a few minutes, he saw Amy enter the room and take a seat at the table, thank goodness. She could cover off for most of it and if questions were asked she couldn't handle at least, he'd get a chance to do that later.

He hoped.

He could only watch the rest of the meeting play out. At a snail's pace, seconds crept on like minutes. The noise in his home had steadily risen in volume until the meeting's audio was drowned out completely.

When Amy and the guys in the meeting rose from their chairs for a short bio-break, Peter bounded to his feet. He raced to the living room where his sound system now blasted out Credence Clearwater Revival. Not bothering with any dials or buttons, he yanked the power plug from the electrical outlet. Next stop was a re-set on the microwave. He pulled the plug from that as well. He didn't think it would stop Liam, but maybe it would slow the son-of-a-gun down.

He leaned against the counter, steadying himself and gulping air. This was insane! How could they carry on any kind of normal life when that horrible ghost continued with his high jinks?

The electrician would be there the next morning, but a simple electrical issue wasn't causing the havoc he was experiencing. He took a deep breath and closed his eyes at his next thought. That left the ghostbuster option to deal with this problem.

He glanced at the clock on the oven and slumped lower. It was time to go back to the meeting. But he couldn't risk partaking audibly, not with that damned ghost playing tricks. He grabbed his cell phone when he sat down in the family room once more. A quick glance at the monitor showed that the meeting had not resumed yet. He hit the dial button to connect to Amy at the office, but dead air was the only answer.

Holding it before his eyes, the icon showed that the battery level of the phone had dropped to one percent. Damn it! This had to be Liam again! It was a nightly ritual of Peter's, charging his cell phone. He was sure it was a full one hundred percent that morning.

Movement on the monitor caught Peter's attention. Amy, and the others in the meeting entered the room and took their seats around the boardroom table. He straightened, looking into the laptop camera with what he hoped was an interested, yet calm expression.

The monitor flickered a few times and then went black. Peter cursed under his breath and got up to check the connections and the power outlet. Everything was secure.

He returned to the laptop and clicked the mouse over the web-link. Still nothing. The internet icon showed that the connection was strong. This was crazy! There was absolutely no reason that the monitor had gone blank, but he couldn't connect even to view it on the laptop screen.

"Liam! Damn it! Quit screwing around! You're messing with my job, man!"

Immediately the screen filled with the scene in the boardroom at work. Peter blew out a huff of air as he rounded the small table to take a seat again. He was barely settled before the Aloe-Vera plant on the table near the window began to rattle against the surface.

Peter jerked back, seeing it vibrate, clacking against the wood. It flew from the table and smashed on the floor about three feet from where it had sat. Green spikes of the plant could be seen in the mound of dirt and the shards of the pot.

Oh, my god. His heart leapt into his throat seeing the pile of debris. Even more unsettling than the fact it had toppled on its own was the fact it had flown a few feet as if something had thrown it.

His gaze darted back to the meeting in progress, trying to look as normal as he could for the camera. But it was hard not to keep his eyes from darting over to the plant and over the room. Whatever.... Whoever—who is he trying to kid? Liam—was still in the room with him.

The ghost had definitely not liked it when he'd yelled at it. The heap of destroyed Aloe Vera on the floor was proof of that.

The meeting couldn't end soon enough.

THIRTEEN

While Peter scrambled to shut the cacophony of noise in their home, Sharon indulged herself with a cookie, listening to Lillian in the library.

"Aunt Mary was just a little girl when the Gallaghers lived in your home. She was only six or seven at that time. She didn't really know much about the parents, but she remembered their daughter, Rose. She was a real beauty and friendly with everyone. There was also an older brother who was crippled with polio. This would be around 1940." Lillian folded her arms over her chest and sighed. "Sorry, Sharon. I'm afraid that doesn't help much regarding Liam."

Sharon shook her head, "No. As you said she was a little girl. I just thought there might be stories she'd heard about his death—especially if the drowning was suspicious."

"Yes." Lillian's eyes narrowed, "Aunt Mary remembered the people who ran the general store, though. Pratt was their name."

"Pratt?" Sharon's eyebrows arched high. "Oh, my God. Descendants of the Pratt family have moved back to Westport.

I met James and Sandy just the other day! They're doing all kinds of renovations to the old homestead."

"Whoa. The house on Main Street? Of course. I've seen the carpenter and electric vans parked there. I hope they have better luck than the original Pratts." Lillian brushed the cookie crumbs from her lap and stood up.

"Why? What happened to the first Pratts?"

"Aunt Mary wasn't sure why it happened, but people stopped buying from them. It was a fifteen minute car ride to Newboro, but she remembers her parents making that trip rather than buy goods from the Pratt's store. They shut the place down after a year or so and moved away."

"That's odd. If this was in the 1940's, that was when World War Two was happening."

Lillian nodded. "I know what you're getting at. During the war, food and gasoline were being rationed. It made little sense to drive to Newboro for weekly groceries."

"For sure. It sounds like the town turned on them. I wonder why." Thinking of the Pratts, Sharon pulled out her phone to check the time. She'd have just enough time before going home to pop by to see how James was doing after his accident. But she wouldn't mention what she'd learned from Lillian about James' ancestors.

"Thanks for the cookies, Sharon! You really didn't have to do that; I enjoyed helping you the other day. If Aunt Mary remembers anything else, I'll call you. She said she was going to call Uncle Frank to see if he remembers anything. He's a few years older, and in a nursing home, so it's a toss up."

Sharon picked up her purse and smiled at Lillian, "I made some headway with the cemetery search. Peter and I are going there later today. It might be just seeing a gravestone, but there might be something more we learn. Who knows?" She turned and before going through the doorway, she waved goodbye. "See you later."

Starting the car, she frowned. It wasn't much, but now she knew from Lillian's aunt that Liam had two children—Rose, a pretty daughter and a son who had been crippled with polio.

The thing with the Pratt's was an odd but interesting item, but wasn't much help with her current predicament, dealing with Liam's ghost.

She parked the car on the street in case any of the workers with the vans parked in the driveway needed to leave. This time when she knocked on the door, Sandy opened it and welcomed her in with a wide grin. "Sharon! I'm sorry about yesterday, but—"

"No need to apologize. Actually, that's why I stopped by. How is James' hand?" She noticed two guys installing drywall in an enormous room to her left. "I don't envy you living with the dust from that."

Sandy nodded, "It's a good thing that we're got everything we need on the second floor. I think that room was originally the store that James's grandparents ran. I'm not sure what we'll do with it; maybe open an art gallery or tea room."

Sharon looked past the workers to a window overlooking the backyard and lake. A quick scan of the room showed that it took up most of the downstairs—large enough for a country store in the 1940's. It would make a picturesque gallery or shop.

She followed Sandy up a wide set of oak stairs leading to their living area. The smell of fresh paint filled the air while sunshine poured into the room from the spacious windows overlooking Big Rideau Lake. James sat before a monitor at a desk in the corner of the room. His hand was wrapped in a white bandage.

Sandy nudged Sharon, murmuring, "He had to get ten stitches. He's sulking because I put my foot down about doing anything more to help with the renovations."

James looked over and waved his wounded hand, greeting Sharon. "It wasn't as bad as Sandy makes out. Just a silly accident with a nail sticking out where it shouldn't have been."

"And only the fifth time you hurt yourself working here." Sandy threw a look at Sharon, "He's so anxious to have all this done...maybe too anxious from all the mishaps he's had. He's amazing on ice and he's not half bad with computer programs.

James was about to get a promotion in the Information Systems Department before we decided to throw in the towel with Toronto."

"So that's what he did after the hockey thing didn't pan out?"

Sandy nodded. "Actually, James hedged his bets on making a career with the Leafs. He took programming in school, just in case. I worked at Sun Life Insurance's head office and got him hired there. But... now we're here!"

Sharon could see the concern and affection in Sandy's eyes when she gazed at James. The poor woman was genuinely worried about her husband's health tackling these renovations. Sharon looked over at James and on impulse, "Would you mind having a look at my website, James? It's for the B&B. I worked on it the other day but I think it needs something. If you feel up to it, that is?" Maybe it would give him something to do and away from the renovations.

He nodded. "Sure. If you send me the link, I'll look at it later." The smile fell from his face, "There's not much else I can do here. It's so frustrating, I could scream." He grabbed a pencil and paper and scribbled something. "Here's my email." He rose and walked over to hand it to Sharon.

"Thanks! That's awfully nice of you, James. It'll be later this evening though. Peter and I have an errand to do." She slipped the paper in her purse. "Speaking of which, I'd better get going. He worked from home today and should be finished with his meeting by now."

As the two women walked down the stairs, Sandy smiled. "Thanks for stopping by. It's a nice break for us from the painting... and each other."

Sharon hid her surprise at Sandy's comment. "Renovations are stressful. I'm sure it's hard on both of you, wanting everything to be finished. I know I would be anxious living through this."

Sandy opened the door and her smile was wistful, "Yes. But it's also that I miss our friends in Toronto. Since we've been here, it's basically just the two of us. I'm looking forward to getting a job just to give us both a break. Opening up some kind of store on the main floor would provide some outside conversation with folks... and an income."

"I'll bet you'll be great working with people, Sandy. But what about James? He seems like more of a loner than a people person." Sharon noticed Sandy's eyes flash wider, and she wondered if she shouldn't have made that comment about James.

"James wasn't always this distant with others. When he was trying out for the team, he got along okay. When he played in college, I don't know how many parties we went to with the other guys and their girlfriends. Even during tryout camp we got together with the other players. But when it didn't pan out, James kind of holed up inside of himself. He couldn't wait to get out of Toronto." She smiled, "I think this move will be good for him. But until this is all done... it's tense sometimes." The look in her eyes showed that there was a lot of 'tense' in her life.

"I hear you. Things will work out though." Sharon said goodbye and walked to her car. Peter had called it right about James. The failure in making the hockey team weighed on him. Living with him couldn't be easy on Sandy. It might be a nice break for the couple if she and Peter had them over for dinner some night. She'd ask Peter about that.

Ten minutes later Sharon parked the car in her driveway. She was about to get out when the gate flew open and Peter appeared. It wasn't just that his face was pale; his movements were fast and jerky, closing the gate and rushing to the car.

When the passenger door opened and he hopped in, she could only stare at him waiting to hear what had upset him.

"That bloody Liam! He did everything he could to disrupt my meeting! First, it was footsteps clomping around upstairs. He screwed around with the microwave, and then the CD player at a million decibels blasting music! I had to pretend my computer was acting up, muting the sound from my end!" Peter's face was tight and he was yelling.

"Oh no. That must have been awful! What are we going to

do?" Sharon slipped her hand around his wrist, rubbing it softly to calm him down.

"I'll tell you what I'll do! When I find his grave, I'm going to pee on it! He may think this is funny, but Shar, it's my job! I'll never be able to do a meeting from home again. Not as long as that jerk is there."

Oh, my God. She'd never seen Peter as angry as he was in that moment. And he had every right to feel that way with what had happened.

Still, the thought of him peeing on Liam's grave, from a guy normally so polite and restrained, was a little comical. She bit down on her lip to keep from laughing, but the chuckles in her throat got out, anyway. She covered her mouth with her hand, trying hard to hold it back.

"Sharon!" He snapped the seatbelt into the holder and glared at her. "By the way, he smashed your aloe plant."

"What? The one your mother gave me?" She had nursed that plant back to life and now it was destroyed? The chuckles turned to shock. That rotten Liam!

"Exactly. Now can we get out of this looney bin for a little while? We have to get someone in to deal with this." He watched her start the car and his tone softened. "I think it's best to postpone booking any overnight guests until this is cleared up."

"Yes, I came to the same decision. We can't have people in with this ghost acting up." She shook her head and backed out of the driveway. "Listen to us. We're discussing a ghost terrorizing our home like he's a teenager acting out. Why won't he leave? What is keeping him here in this plane of existence?"

"Maybe he doesn't realize that he's dead. Or maybe the only place he could move on to is the fire and brimstone one."

She glanced over at him as they drove down the street, "You don't believe in hell. Neither do I. But there's definitely something keeping him here. Why else would he stay when he would have the chance to 'go into the light'?"

The rest of the way to the cemetery on the hill on the outskirts of the village was spent in silence. A quick glance at

Peter showed that he was still shook up with what had happened during his meeting.

Hopefully, there'd be something they'd find out at his gravestone.

FOURTEEN

Sharon found the gravestone after threading slowly through the rows of headstones. It was a large granite slab; the surname, Gallagher was etched in stark relief. A quick glance at the script below showed the first name, Liam F.

She scanned the plot of land looking for Peter and saw him stooped, examining the worn carvings of other headstones with his hands clasped behind his back. "Peter! Over here! I found it."

Turning back to the stone, she read…

In loving memory of Liam Gallagher, died
November 1, 1943 at 52 years
His wife Elizabeth "Ginny" Brown died Jan 17,
1953 aged 59 years
Son Sean 1927-1981
Daughter Rose 1929-1996

Her eyes narrowed, taking in the gravestone's appearance. The search through the cemetery had revealed many weathered ancient stones where the inscriptions denoting the deceased were difficult to read. Yet the carvings on this stone were so fresh looking it could have been put up yesterday.

Bending over, reading the monument, Peter said, "It looks like the whole family's buried here. Did any of his kids marry? You'd expect them to be buried with their own spouses."

Sharon shrugged. "Yeah, they must have never married." She pointed at the headstone. "You see anything strange about that headstone?"

"Nope. Looks fine to me."

She shook her head and pointed to another headstone nearby. "Look at that one there. The year of death on that one is 1949. It's pretty much the same style as Liam's, right?"

"Sure. Probably the same guy did both. I doubt there were many headstone companies in this area back then, right?"

"Right! But that one's pretty worn, isn't it? It's not easy to read the inscription, right?"

Peter nodded, and turned back to Liam's family plot. "Waitaminnit. Liam's headstone looks brand new, but that one's worn..." he turned to Sharon. "You trying to say there's something weird about the headstone?" He shook his head. "No way, Sharon. No freaking way."

Sharon knew she was on to something. "I think 'way' honey." She stepped up to the monument and crouched to look at the engravings closely. Liam's name showed slight score marks, like those a hammer and chisel would produce. But when she looked at the names of his children, they were perfectly carved.

She gave a quick nod and stood up. "Liam's name was hand carved onto this stone. The names of his children were sand-blasted on, Peter." She tapped the top of the slab. "This has been here since 1943 and hasn't aged a bit!"

The shivering tingle that ran up her spine told her she was right.

"What the hell are you trying to say?" Peter asked. His voice was at a higher pitch. Any higher and Sharon knew he'd be squeaking. "The guy is dead and buried, okay?"

"Yeah, but he hasn't moved on. And somehow, this headstone is evidence."

Peter trembled a bit. "That definitely creeps me out, Sharon." He looked up to the sky. "Like the pranks during my meeting weren't enough! I don't know why, but this is even weirder than the aloe plant getting smashed."

Sharon stepped up to him and took his hand. "I know exactly what you mean." She looked over at the headstone again. "Poor Ginny—a widow for ten years... that's sad."

"Humph. Maybe not for her. It's possible that she finally had some peace in her life, if what's happening in our home is any sign of his character."

Sharon gave him a soft jab in the ribs. "We're standing at his grave, Peter. Try to show some respect for the dead."

Peter stared hard at the dirt before the gravestone. "Liam Gallagher your bones are under my feet. So are your wife's and your kids'. You must have loved your family. Why would you not want to be with them in the afterlife?"

Sharon noticed that his cheeks had become slightly flushed and his hands were thrust deep in his pockets. She slipped her arm through his and leaned into him. "That's honest." She continued Peter's train of thought, "Liam, you need to go to your wife and Rose and Sean. You don't belong in our house anymore. There's nothing there for you. No one who loves you like your family. Please, if any part of you is listening, please leave our house in peace."

Peter looked down at her when she finished. "I sincerely hope that this works." He scuffed the grass with the toe of his sneaker and bent down, scratching a bit of soil into his hand. "I'm taking this soil from his grave home with us. Just in case he has a hard time believing us that he's actually dead. This is proof."

Sharon's eyebrows lifted, and she nodded. "That's not a bad idea. I've read that sometimes spirits linger when they die because their death was sudden and unexpected. They have a hard time processing the fact that they've died." At that point she was ready to try anything to get Liam to move on. Soil from his grave might help convince Liam that he didn't belong with the living any longer.

Peter nudged her, and they started walking back to where they'd parked the car. Before they got very far, Peter stopped and called over his shoulder, "If you don't get the message and I have to come back here again, I'm definitely going to pee on your grave, Liam. That's a promise. Sorry for your relatives, but you will have bought and paid for it."

Sharon yanked his arm, "Peter! That's not funny!" She looked up at him, but the corners of her mouth twitched when she spoke, "Honestly. I don't know who's the bigger jackass here—you or Liam."

"Hey! He started it! He wrecked my meeting! I'll be lucky if I don't get fired!"

"What a child you are!" Despite her rebuke, Sharon couldn't help but smile at Peter's protests.

Peter put his arm around her shoulders and hugged her to his body as they walked to the car. "What's for supper, Shar?"

***

When they got home Peter put the soil from the gravesite on a piece of white paper. Turning to Sharon, "I think we need to go from room to room showing this to him. That way we will get the message across."

"Let me. I think he likes me more than he likes you." She couldn't help thinking of the gentle touch on her face that first night in the house; it was almost a caress. Add that to the snippets of that fuzzy feeling she'd experienced since she'd arrived, and the other sensations she'd experienced, she knew she had a stronger connection to the supernatural than Peter did.

She took the sheet of paper, folding it slightly to prevent any spilling onto her clean floors. For the next fifteen minutes they wandered from room to room, with Sharon repeating her message. "Liam Gallagher, I am sorry to tell you that this soil is from the grave where you, your wife and children lay. They have passed on and it's time you joined them. Go in peace and love." All the while she did this, there was a heaviness in her chest; a soft pang of sorrow, loss and grief worked around the edges of her heart.

The finality, seeing the gravestone where the entire family was buried and the fact that Liam was stuck in some kind of limbo, playing tricks in the home where he'd lived and loved his family struck her as sad and lonesome.

When they finally finished and went to the kitchen to make dinner, Sharon could see the same sense of melancholy in Peter that she was feeling. There was also a sense of hope that their ritual would also free Liam. The air in her home seemed clearer. The last rays of the sun flowed over the hardwood floors and onto the gleaming granite countertops.

"What are we going to do with the soil, now?" Sharon handed the paper to her husband.

"I thought I'd add it to the aloe-vera dirt. I'm going to clean that mess right now."

Sharon's eyes became wider. "No! You can't do that! Potting him with a houseplant? It's... it's sacrilegious. He'll definitely stay to haunt us if you do that!"

Peter rolled his eyes, "So what do you suggest? We get an urn and put it on the mantle?"

"No! But you can't put him in the aloe plant. I'll put it in an envelope and seal it. It belongs with our house papers, if nothing else." She left him standing in the kitchen and marched up the stairs to find an envelope.

She had barely filed it away when her cell phone dinged.

A quick glance at the screen showed Lillian's name. Eagerly she brushed the icon to answer. Before she even had a chance to say hello, Lillian's voice burst through.

"Sharon? Oh, my god! Wait till you hear what Aunt Mary found out from Uncle Frank. I'm coming over!"

FIFTEEN

Sharon zipped into the kitchen where Peter was at the sink peeling potatoes. He asked her, "Would you rather have green beans or carrots with dinner?"

She grasped his arm, "We need to put supper off. Lillian from the library just called. She's on her way over to see us. Apparently her uncle told her some things about Liam and his family."

Peter paused and his eyes widened as she talked. "Sure. That's not a problem. To be honest, I'm not all that hungry. I wonder what she found out." He plopped the potato in the waiting pot and set it on the back burner of the stove.

"I have no idea, but she sounded excited. I'll make some tea and we can put cookies out." Sharon hardly had the words out before there was a knock on their front door.

Peter nudged her. "I'll make the tea. You answer the door, Shar."

She practically ran to greet Lillian. When she opened the door, Lillian blurted, "I just realized the time. I hope I'm not interrupting your dinner or anything. But I knew you'd want to know what Aunt Mary learned from Uncle Frank."

Sharon stood aside and waved Lillian in. "You're not interrupting. We just got back from the cemetery." Sharon led the way to the kitchen where Peter stood waiting. "Peter, this is Lillian Babcock." She smiled at Lillian, "Lillian, my husband, Peter."

What was so important that Lillian would want to speak to them in person?

"Have a seat, Lillian. We've just put the kettle on for some tea. I can't wait to hear what your uncle told your aunt. Does he live in Westport?" Sharon waited until Lillian was settled before taking a seat across from her.

Lillian folded her hands together resting them on the table. "No. He's actually older than Aunt Mary. He's in a nursing home in Kingston." She chuckled, "Aunt Mary said he probably couldn't tell you what he had for breakfast that day but he can recall things from years ago, clear as a bell."

"Sounds like me." Peter sat down next to Sharon. "So he had memories of Liam or at least knew the stories going round about his death?"

Lillian nodded. "Uncle Frank is six years older than Mary. He remembered the same thing she did about the Pratts—that people stopped going to the store—but he knew part of the reason. One thing was that the Pratts were kind of snobbish. That only changed on Sundays when they made a grand show of being at church, glad-handing everyone."

Sharon snickered, "I know the type."

Lillian rolled her eyes and smiled, "Yeah. Well, he remembered one time when he was a boy overhearing his parents talking about Liam Gallagher and how he died. It was late in the evening and Uncle Frank had got up to use the bathroom." She made a quick smile. "That man's memory... he recalled that he'd eaten too many fresh apples that day and had a case of the trots at night."

Sharon nodded, smiling, "You said he had great recall of days gone by..."

Lillian continued, "When he was passing near the kitchen his parents were at the kitchen table talking. They didn't see him and he heard them talking about the Gallaghers—how poor Ginny had to take in boarders to make ends meet after Liam drowned. Uncle Frank remembered his dad's remark, 'Drowning, or was drowned on purpose, you mean.' Well Uncle Frank's ears perked up at that and he stayed quiet, listening to the rest of the conversation."

Sharon leaned closer, "So that letter was right. But why? Even if Liam had pulled some prank, that would hardly be reason enough to want him dead. That's extreme, if you ask me."

"I'd agree... except for what else Uncle Frank remembered." Lillian leaned over the table, fixing them both with a wide-eyed look, "Pratt wasn't above pressing his thumb on the scale when weighing grains or meat. Everyone suspected it, but it took someone like Liam Gallagher to point it out. The day it happened, an old lady was buying something and Liam called Pratt out on it. He made a bit of a to-do about it. When Pratt told the woman how much she owed, Liam made him re-weigh it and told him to keep his hands in his pockets. Turned out he charged the poor woman for almost a whole extra pound! Liam tried to make a joke of it—he said that Pratt had 'thick old thumbs' or something. Pratt got really angry and threw Liam out of the store."

"What a jerk! And your uncle remembered all this? That's amazing." Peter let out a long sigh and pushed away from the table.

Lillian watched him, adding, "It became a standing joke in the village. 'Thick thumb Pratt' was what my uncle said. That's what they started to call him, and Pratt hated that. Which, of course, helped in keeping the joke going." Lillian shrugged. "It was another time, and that's what people did back then. But if Pratt was fleecing people, who could blame them?"

Sharon had been listening closely, picturing what that must have been like. She commented, "There explains the bad blood between the Pratts and the Gallaghers."

"Looks like it." Lillian slapped the table to punctuate her remark. "There was bad blood between the Pratts and the

Gallaghers. Uncle Frank also said that the Pratts never showed any remorse when Liam died. They never even went to his funeral, although practically the whole village turned out for it. That turned people off. Especially when Liam left a widow to raise a teenage girl on her own and saddled with a crippled son at home too."

When the kettle began whistling, Peter stood. "I'll get the tea. You'll have a cup, won't you, Lillian?"

"Absolutely! Thanks, Peter."

But Sharon barely heard their words. After a moment she asked the question that had been pinging around in her brain, "Did your uncle think the Pratts had anything to do with Liam's death?"

CRASH!

"Damn it!"

When Sharon spun to see what happened, the kettle was on the floor, boiling water covering the surface where Peter stepped gingerly, "What happened?" She rose to grab the tea towel to help soak up the water.

"I don't know. I should have used a pot holder, I guess." He stood at the sink, running cold water over his hand. "The handle was hot as blazes. That shouldn't have happened."

Using a pot holder, Sharon put the kettle in the sink to cool and mopped up the spilled water with a dishtowel.

"Can I help you, Sharon?"

She looked over at Lillian. "No. I'll get this cleaned up in a flash." As she mopped and squeezed the water from the drenched towel she couldn't help thinking, 'Just when we were talking about Liam's death and the Pratts, the kettle burns Peter's hand.'

"Never mind the tea, Sharon. Don't make it on my account." Lillian rose and grabbed a handful of paper towels from the roll. "How's your hand, Peter?"

"The icy water is helping. I'll be fine in a minute or two."

Sharon finished the last of her section of the floor near the counter and took the wet towels from the other woman. "That's interesting what your aunt found out, Lillian. It explains how the Pratts became social Pariahs."

Peter mumbled, "I wouldn't pass that along to Sandy and James though. It happened so long ago that it doesn't matter now. No sense upsetting them."

"No. I won't. You're right."

THUD!

The floor shook under Sharon's feet even though the banging came from upstairs. She gasped and stood still as a statue, gaping at Peter and Lillian.

Lillian looked up at the ceiling as if she expected to see a branch poking through. "Oh, my God. What was that? I hope a tree limb didn't fall on the house."

"Nope. I think I know what caused that." Peter marched out of the kitchen while Sharon followed at his heels.

When they reached the bottom of the main staircase leading to their room upstairs, the envelope that Sharon had tucked away with the dirt from Liam's grave was ripped in two and the earth of the gravesite was scattered across the floor.

Peter's arm shot out holding Sharon back, "Stay here! I'll go up and see what happened." He bounded up the stairs, taking them two at a time.

"What on earth?"

Sharon jerked at Lillian's voice beside her. She turned to her new friend. "What on earth is pretty accurate. That's soil we took from Liam's gravesite. It was supposed to show him he's dead and to convince him to pass on to the other realm. But instead, he's using it to send us a nasty message."

"Oh, my." Lillian's hand rose to her chest, and she took a deep breath.

"Are you okay, Lillian?" Sharon leaned closer, watching her blink fast a few times. When a wide smile soon appeared on Lillian's face, Sharon felt her own chest ease.

"I'm fine! This is the most exciting thing that's happened to me in many, many years! Don't get me wrong; it's creepy as hell and I don't envy you living here."

Peter's shout, "Sharon?" caused both of the women to peer up the stairs. When he followed up in a softer tone with "You need to see this." Sharon bounded up the staircase with Lillian on her heels.

Sharon jerked back when she saw the mess in her bedroom. She was barely conscious of Lillian standing peering over her shoulder. The metal filing cabinet was completely upended, perched against the wall with the drawers yawning open. In the center of the room was a scattered heap of files, the office chair beside them.

"Oh, my goodness. Did he—the ghost—do that?" Lillian whispered.

In reply, the office chair began to slowly spin on its own. The three of them watched in stunned silence as it spun faster and faster.

"STOP IT LIAM!" Sharon screamed.

The chair abruptly stilled.

Peter sniffed the air. "Do you smell anything?"

"That's pipe tobacco," Lillian said. She sniffed again. "Prince Albert cherry, I think…"

"Yeah," Sharon added.

Peter threaded his fingers through his hair, staring down at the mess. It was hard to tell if he was more angry or defeated. "Shar, we need help to deal with this. Call the… you know, the medium or sensitives or what these ghostbuster characters go by. This has got to stop."

But that wasn't what made Sharon's blood go cold. It was that chair. Her chair. It spun again, slowly, and stopped again.

It was that more than any other thing that had happened that afternoon that filled her with a sense of dread.

Liam was there in the room with them, and he wanted them to know it.

The chair began to slowly revolve again…

SIXTEEN

"Stop it right now Liam!" Sharon raced to the chair and grasped the backrest, her fingers clawing at the leather. Finally, the damned thing came to a halt. Her heart pounded while her breath came out in a fast pant. For a moment a wave of dizziness flooded through her body and she stepped quickly to the side, trying to catch her balance. The tingling was coursing through her entire body, not just up her back.

Immediately Peter was next to her, pulling her into him and holding her close. "It's okay. We'll fix this, Shar."

Tears burned the back of Sharon's eyes and she took a deep breath through teeth clenched so hard they rasped like two bricks rubbing together. This was wrong, so very wrong and unfair! She'd lost a career and wanted to follow this dream in her dream home and this ghost, *this bastard* was ruining everything! He'd even tried to wreck Peter's meeting, threatening his career. Hell, he was scaring the daylights out of her and Peter, not to mention Lillian who stood frozen in the doorway.

She pushed away from her husband and peered about the

room. Her fingernails bit into the palm of her hands when she cried out to the ceiling, "What do you want with us? We didn't do anything to you! You need to leave this house. You're dead and I'm sorry about that, but you can't stay here anymore. GO!"

Movement in the periphery of her line of sight caught her attention. The corner of the curtain fluttered and then billowed high before falling to shimmer slightly. It could have been a breeze from outside, but when Sharon felt the gossamer touch on her cheek, she knew it was Liam. A cool brush of air beside her ear made her skin prickle even before she heard, *'Ginny'* whispered faintly.

The tears she'd been fighting trickled down her cheeks and she squeezed her eyes shut. A vision flooded her mind of the two people who had once shared this room. A tall man with weathered lines etched in his face holding the hand of a shorter, portly woman with ebony hair. The outpouring of love and sorrow in the man's eyes as he gazed at his Ginny was heartbreaking. He had disappointed her and desperately wanted things to be right between them again. Her shoulders wracked as the maelstrom of emotions flowed through her. It could never be right between the old couple again.

"Sharon?"

Her eyes flew open when Peter gripped her upper arms, giving her a firm shake. It took a moment to focus, to see the concern in his eyes.

"I... I saw him. It was just a glimmer. Oh Peter, I could feel the love he felt for his wife. I could see her too, just for a fraction of a second." Her fingertips grazed her earlobe. "He spoke. He whispered, 'Ginny' right next to my ear."

She searched Peter's face for any sign that he believed her. But only worry etched in the deep furrow between his eyebrows showed.

"Sharon? You really saw him?" Lillian had wandered over and now stood a few inches away, peering at her.

"Yes!" When Peter's hands fell from her arms, she reached to swipe the tears from her eyes. "Peter, I saw Liam and

Ginny! But Ginny isn't responsible for any of this. It's Liam! He's here and I think he's confused. I could feel the love that he still feels for her." Oh, my God! The loneliness and grief that had surrounded Liam tore through her heart.

The look of disbelief in Peter's eyes gave way to worry. "Sharon? How is that possible?"

Lillian spoke again. "You really saw him, Sharon? You saw this Liam guy and his wife? Has anything like this ever happened to you before, I mean seeing spirits?"

Sharon took a deep breath and her gaze fell to the floor. She hadn't liked the 'cursed gift'; sensing supernatural things when she'd been a child and she liked it even less now. But this house and Liam had other plans.

She looked over at Lillian and Peter, "I saw my grandmother after she had died. But that was when I was a child. Only eight. I told you about that, Peter. Remember?"

"Sure. But you were a kid."

Sharon took a deep breath. "There was other stuff..."

Peter cocked his head. In a gentle voice, he said, "What other stuff, babe?"

Sharon sighed. "When I was a kid, I could... sense things. If something was lost, I knew where it was." She looked at Peter and to Lillian. "I could tell people's secrets, just by touching them." She swallowed. "And once... I had a vision."

Lillian gasped. "A vision?"

"Yes. I envisioned my father getting into a horrible car wreck. He had to go work and I had that vision. It scared the hell out of me." She looked at both of them. "So I hid his car keys." She grimaced. "He went crazy looking for them. When I knew the danger had passed, the next day, I gave them to him."

Peter scoffed. "That must have gone over well."

"Oh man, he was sooo furious! He told me I was going to be grounded for a million years! I tried to explain to him why, and that only made him angrier. Until..."

"What?" Lillian and Peter said in unison.

"When he finally left to head to work, he passed a huge car

wreck! There must have been five cars involved! Two people were killed, and one of the cars was exactly like I described—a cherry red sports car."

Peter took her hand. "Does this still go on with you?"

She shook her head. "No. All that stopped..." she glanced at Lillian, "when I went through puberty." She took a breath. "But now... I think it's back."

Peter nodded slowly. "I remember you telling me about your grandmother. But in all the years we've been together, this is the first time I've ever seen anything like this happen to you. You were in some kind of trance just now, Sharon."

Sharon's fingers threaded through her hair and then fisted a handful. "I know! God, it was so real!" Turning to Lillian, her voice softened, "After my family moved to Niagara, the dreams and premonitions ended. And then there was high school and all that teenage drama." She looked up at Peter, "So why now?"

"I think it's this house, Sharon. Moving here, to a house that's haunted by this Liam character, brought it all back. You had those episodes when you were a child; it's only natural that with what's been going on in this house that any 'sensitivity' you have would come to life."

Lillian stroked Sharon's back and gazed at her. "I've read about small children who see relatives who have passed on. They can describe them to a 'T' even though they'd never met them. A few cases could point out the dead relative from old photos. But then, whatever supernatural gift they have just goes away as they grow older. Sounds like what happened to you, Sharon."

That was it exactly. Sharon sighed, wondering about the next thing that would happen with Liam. She was exhausted. How much more could she take before she had to give up on this house, this dream of opening a B&B? Was it worth her sanity? Peter's sanity?

As if she sensed the despair in Sharon, Lillian offered to help Peter clean up the mess in the small office area. "You sit down. Sharon. We'll get this tidied and then we'll have that cup of tea. I think you need it."

Sharon slumped over to the bed and sat down, watching them scoop up papers and put the file cabinet back where it belonged. "I think something stronger is in order, Lillian. I need a stiff drink of brandy."

Peter managed to slide the cabinet back to its original place and then he smiled at Sharon, "We all need a stiff drink, Sharon. It's been a day."

***

A half an hour later, the three of them sat at the kitchen table nursing brandy. Sharon had lost her appetite for dinner, preferring to drink it instead of eat it. The brandy worked its magic, settling into her muscles until she felt numb and even a little mellow. "I wonder if seeing Liam, sensing his pain and love, is related to this stage in my life. You know, I had sensitivities as a child and now going through..." Her fingers hooked making air quotes, "... 'the change', has brought it all on again."

Peter topped up their glasses and looked over at her. "But that doesn't explain what happened today during my meeting. It's not just you, Sharon. We're all experiencing this guy's pranks."

Lillian waved a hand at him. "I don't think so. Liam has done pranks to you, but Sharon's the one who saw him."

"And heard him, and felt his touch," Sharon added.

Peter rolled his eyes. "Okay then, you win! Aren't youuuu special!" he gibed. With a glance at Lillian, he continued, "When you told us that the Pratts were ostracized by the town after Liam died... that was when things started in this kitchen. First, I burn myself and then he trashes the office, throwing the dirt from his grave down the stairs for good measure."

Sharon nodded. "Yes, that occurred to me as well. Whatever bad blood there was between Liam and the Pratts is still there." Her eyes grew wide at the next thought. "The descendants of the Pratts move back into the village to their family home and Liam is acting up in what was once his own home. You can't tell me it's a coincidence."

Peter snorted, "There's only one way we'll know if your theory is correct, Shar. We need to call the previous owners to see if Liam made their lives a living hell here. They were here before the younger Pratts moved back." His eyes narrowed, "If they knew this house was haunted and didn't disclose it, then I will really be pissed."

"I'd be surprised if they had any experiences with Liam, hon."

"Why?"

"Just my gut."

He let out an exasperated sigh, "I think we need to call the previous owner and find out what she knows about this. Then the next call is to one of these ghostbuster types. I hate the thought of doing that, but I hate what's happening in this house even more."

Sharon nodded. "I'll call her tomorrow. Maybe we should cancel the electrician's visit as well. It would save money since we are pretty sure who and what is causing the problems with the lights and TV monitor. And the plumbing... that water pressure drop I had in the shower?" She nodded firmly. "I'm thinking Liam."

Lillian had been silently listening to them, but now she spoke. "If your ghost did the damage to your office when we were just talking about the Pratts, what would he do if the Pratts were to visit you here? I mean, they could be out for an evening stroll and just happen to walk by. What kind of tantrum would Liam pull if that happened?"

Sharon looked over at Peter. It wasn't out of the question, not after they'd done pretty well exactly that a couple days before. "It wouldn't be good if James and Sandy ever stopped by. Liam might set the house on fire or something equally bad." She snorted, "Earlier today, I'd thought of asking them for dinner. That ain't happening!"

Peter's eyes narrowed. "Or maybe he'd see that Sandy and James aren't his enemy. His enemy, if it was the elder Pratts are long gone... as Liam should be! It's tempting just to invite them over, just out of spite after all that Liam has put us through."

..e looked up at the ceiling and yelled. "Kidding! Don't trash the office again, okay?"

Lillian let out a short laugh, "I'm glad you added that you're not going to ask them over. At least don't try taunting him until I'm out of here, Peter." She looked at her watch and then continued, "What are you going to do, Sharon? I don't know if you guys are religious but you might consider having a priest in, to bless the house. Maybe that will convince Liam to leave." She rose to her feet. "Speaking of leaving, I need to get back to check on Aunt Mary. I kind of wish I hadn't burst in here with all my news. I ruined your evening. I'm sorry."

Sharon felt like the world was on her shoulders when she pushed away from the table and stood up. "It's not your fault, Lillian. You were shedding more light on the situation, that's all. No. This is on Liam, I'm afraid."

"Well, think about getting the priest in. If you want, I can call him. I sometimes go to church with Aunt Mary, so I kind of know him." Lillian offered as she walked out of the kitchen.

"I might try that. It seems hypocritical, seeing as how we aren't members of his parish, but we're also new here. Maybe we'll have to join." Sharon reached for the door handle to open it for Lillian.

"Try to get some rest, Sharon. Also, have a bite to eat before you go to bed. You'll feel better in the morning. Let me know if there's anything I can do to help out here. I feel terrible that you're going through this." Lillian patted Sharon's shoulder and then left.

When Sharon returned to the kitchen, Peter set a plate of cheese and crackers on the table. He'd taken the bottle of brandy away and replaced it with a jug of milk. She plopped down into the chair and poured a glass. "My stomach will thank you for this in the morning."

Peter took a seat across from her. "I don't want to leave you alone here, tomorrow. But after the screw-up with the meeting, I need to go in. But I'll leave work early, I promise."

Sharon shook her head. "I'll be fine. You do what you have to do and don't worry about me. Believe it or not, what happened earlier, sensing Liam and his wife may be a good thing. At least I know more about him. I felt his pain and loneliness. Which is why I can't understand why he's still here. What does he get out of hanging around a house where he lived with his family, when it's occupied by strangers? It can't be just wanting to get revenge on the Pratts."

"Maybe you're giving him too much credit. You're looking at this logically while he doesn't operate like that at all. He's played tricks on us, but what happened this evening showed actual anger, like a child having a tantrum."

Sharon had to agree, especially since it was the second time they'd had to clean the office because of Liam. She shook her head slowly, trying to make sense of all they'd learned that night. "But I can't believe that the elder Pratts murdered Liam. It just seems so over the top. They were just shopkeepers, not mafia types."

"Well, that second hand info from Lillian's not much evidence is it?" He leaned back. "I mean, she's telling a story her aunt heard from an even older relative that happened a looong time ago, right? Pretty thin."

"Maybe he carried a prank too far? I was so angry at him upstairs, right? Maybe he carried a prank too far and someone wanted to get even."

Peter shrugged. "Someone like the Pratts?" He picked a piece of cheese from the plate and popped it into his mouth. "Well, until we know more about the history or we can convince Liam to leave, let's hope that James and Sandy Pratt stay well away from this house."

Sharon took a deep breath, "Or, it may be the catalyst, the breakthrough that we need to convince Liam to leave. He may not like it but it will show him that life has moved on without him. He'll see that he is wrong, that being here is wrong—kind of like shock therapy to get through to him."

"I don't think that's a good idea. And as nice as it was that Lillian offered to introduce us to her minister, it seems too hypocritical of us to join her church just to get the minister's blessing. I'd rather go the ghostbuster route, to be honest."

"I'll meet you halfway. As far as getting a medium in... I think that will make things worse. It would be one more stranger trying to communicate with him, invading his home. He showed himself to me, tonight. There is kind of a relationship between us. If this 'gift' has returned to me, I might be the best person to deal with him."

Peter sat back in the chair and crossed his arms over his chest. "You know I support you in whatever you decide. We disagree on the Pratts and the shock therapy angle, but ultimately it's your call. This house, trying your hand at a B&B means a lot to you. I won't stand in your way."

She leaned across the table and held her hand out. When he took it in both of his, she smiled at him. "Thanks. I appreciate your support, Peter. I've got a feeling that this is the best way to get some peace in this house, so we can live our lives. I'm not running away from this. This is our home, not Liam's anymore."

SEVENTEEN

Later that night, Sharon snuggled into Peter when they settled in bed. "If you die before me, would you hang around to be with me?"

His hand rubbed her back, pulling her even closer. "I'd have to. I'd want to be sure that some gigolo didn't latch onto you for the insurance money and blow through it all. I'd have to haunt you, if that happened."

She gave him a playful swat on the chest. "It would be just the money they'd be after, is that it? Thanks a lot! If I die first, I will definitely haunt you!"

"You'd want to nag me about keeping the house clean, right? And for the record, it wouldn't be just the money that would make guys hit on you! You make awesome brownies, Sharon." He grabbed her hand just as she was about to give him another swat. "You know I'm teasing! It's not just your brownies. You make amazing lasagna, too."

He wasn't fast enough when she gave his foot a sharp kick. "Ow! Sorry. You're also an outstanding street fighter, Shar!" He pulled her in closer, pinning her legs and arms so she couldn't hit him again. "You know I'd stay to be with you.

That's the truth. It makes me feel sorry for Liam. Don't get me wrong. He's a total jerk, but he's also kind of pathetic too."

"Yeah. That's kind of why I want to handle this, rather than get some medium in. I feel like I sort of know him, if that makes any sense. I've seen him and he even whispered his wife's name in my ear. Maybe I remind him of her."

Peter reached to turn the bedside lamp off and then snuggled close again. He murmured sleepily, "I'm glad you don't do pottery. I can see it now. I come home and there's Liam holding your hands as the pottery wheel turns. Just like in that movie, *Ghost*."

"You're crazy, Peter, you know that, right?"

He kissed her forehead. "Crazy about you, Sharon. Good night."

It seemed to take a long time before Sharon was able to turn her mind off. She kept reliving that brief moment when she'd seen Liam and Ginny. Finally she drifted off.

***

She was outside in her yard at night. A quick glance at the sky showed bright clouds floating past a crescent moon. The smell of pipe tobacco smoke lingered in the still air around her. At the flash of a small flame, she saw him—a tall black shape, putting the lit match to his pipe and puffing a plume of cherry smelling smoke. It was him! She knew it had to be Liam. When he turned his head to gaze at her, he lowered the pipe and smiled.

"Liam? It's you, isn't it?" She took a step closer, peering at him.

"Aye. And you are the new one. Sharon." He looked up at the sky, watching the moon appear from behind the cloud cover. "A crescent moon, the first quarter. It's smiling at me."

Sharon rubbed her bare arms, wishing she'd grabbed her housecoat before she came outside. But she couldn't remember coming out of the house. The night air was cool and damp and the moist grass chilled her feet as she stepped even closer to him. But as she watched him, the features of his face became clearer from the enhanced light above. Yes, older than she was, but only by a few years. He was almost six feet tall and slender, despite the bulky sweater and baggy pants. The peak of his tweed cap cast a shadow over his eyes, but there was a flash of a twinkle as he looked above.

"Why are you here, Liam?" It was funny that she felt no fear being in his presence. It was as natural as sitting down to breakfast with Peter.

"And why should I not be here? I enjoy the moonlight. You can take your full moons and new moons, even a blue moon. For me, it's always been the crescent moon that's most appealing. It's laughing. Whether at us or with us, I could not say."

"It's pretty. But that isn't what I meant, Liam. Why are you still in this house and in this yard? Your time was long ago. This is my house now." She was so close that she could see his gnarled fingers holding the bowl of the pipe.

"My time or rather my life is here in this home. Ginny's got a bee in her bonnet but she'll get over it. When she does, I'll be here for her." He turned to face Sharon, making her take a step back. "It's ye who shouldn't be here. I promised Ginny I'd always take care of her. That means being here when she returns."

"No, Liam. She's not coming back. Ginny and Rose and Sean are gone. You need to go to them. They want you with them, Liam." She tried to sound as gentle as she could, but he had to know that his family was dead.

"You don't know my Ginny." With that he turned and started walking away, the pipe smoke trailing after him.

"Wait! Where are you going? I need to talk to you, Liam!" She darted after him, but he was now on the other side of the gate.

"The moon is grinning. It's time to pay a wee visit to some folk." And then faded into the shadows of the night.

"No! Come back!" Sharon grasped the handle and tried to open the gate, but it was stuck. She tugged at it, but it wouldn't budge. "Wait! Where are you going?" She'd try climbing over! She had to get to him before...

"Wake up, Sharon!"

She turned and Peter's face peered down at her. What was he doing there? Maybe he could open the gate.

"Sharon! You're having a dream! Wake up!" Peter shook her shoulder, while his eyes bore through her.

"What? Peter!" Her heartbeat thundered in her ears as she jolted awake. When she tried to sit up, Peter's arm went around her, helping her rise higher against the pillow. "I had a dream about Liam, Peter! It was so real! We talked about his wife and kids."

Peter reached for the glass of water on Sharon's nightstand and handed it to her. "Here. Drink this, you're trembling." He took her other hand in his. "Your hand is like ice! Maybe I should get something warm for you to drink."

Sharon finished the water and set the glass on the table. Her hand shook, and she quickly set it in her lap to still. She could feel the dampness of her nightgown. It had to be from a hot flash...right?

"I'm fine, Peter. But the dream... it was so real. I talked to Liam. This kind of thing, a dream so vivid, hasn't happened to me since I was a little girl. I used to have premonitions in my dreams that would puzzle me, but this was different, more intense. I smelled his pipe smoke, saw the glint in his eyes and heard the chuckle in his voice as he remarked on the moon."

"You said you spoke to him about his family? Why won't he join them and leave us the hell alone?" Peter sat down next to her on the bed, watching her closely.

She blinked a few times, reliving the dream in her mind. "He thinks his wife is coming back. It sounded like he and Ginny had a quarrel and that he thinks she's still angry. I told him that his family has died, that they won't be returning. He acted like none of that was true, carrying on with his evening. He left, and that's when I woke up."

"So he didn't believe you. Where was he going? With any luck, he went to the lake where he drowned and he'll stay there." Peter sighed when he glanced at the alarm clock on his side of the bed. "Shit. It's almost five. I'll never get back to sleep knowing the alarm will go off at six. We might as well get up... or do you want to go back to sleep? You don't need to get up."

Sharon placed her hand on his cheek, gazing at him. "I'm sorry. You will be so tired when you get to work. I'll get up and make you some breakfast."

"It will be a long day for you too, Sharon. Maybe you can catch a nap this afternoon. I'll take a shower and then I'll be down." He rose and trudged off to the ensuite bath.

Sharon watched the door close and the slump of her husband's shoulders before he disappeared inside. This was taking a toll on both of them.

She sat there for a few minutes more, reliving the dream in her mind. There was something about the crescent moon that had held Liam's attention. He said it looked like it was grinning. She got out of bed and slipped her robe on before stepping over to the window to peek outside. Gazing up at the sky, her eyes widened seeing the crescent moon above the horizon. And it was the first quarter moon, just like in the dream! When she stepped away, she caught a glimpse of her feet and stopped short. There was a smudge of mud on the outside of her big toe and a smear of green grass near her heel.

Oh, my God.

EIGHTEEN

Sharon didn't mention the dirt and grass stains she'd found on her foot when Peter joined her for breakfast. It just couldn't be possible she'd gone outside during the night. Peter had awakened her just as she was about to follow Liam and she'd been in her own bed. There had to be some other explanation for the stains on her feet. Maybe she'd stepped in the dirt from the grave that Liam had tossed down the stairs. Whatever it was, there was no way she would risk worrying Peter more than he already was.

He finished his coffee and pushed back from the table. "Don't go to any trouble making dinner, Sharon. I'll pick up a pizza on my way home. We'll make it a movie night and hit the hay early."

She poured a second cup of coffee and nodded. "Fine by me. After the electrician leaves, I might try working on my website again and..." Her voice trailed off, and she swore, "Damn it! I was going to send the link to James. He's apparently a whiz with computers and websites, and he said he'd have a look at it. I'll do that after I tidy up the kitchen."

Peter stepped over to her and put his hands on her

shoulders, a gentle look in his eyes. "Don't beat yourself up about it. With all that happened yesterday, I'm surprised you remembered it now. And you didn't exactly get a great night's sleep, what with your dream and all."

"Yeah. I know. I think I need to get out of this house for a while. Maybe I'll go for a hike this afternoon. The fresh air will do me good." Sharon felt every one of her forty-nine years and then some. Dealing with Liam, never knowing when he'd pull something again, was wearing her down. Why couldn't he just leave them in peace?

"That sounds like an excellent idea. When you get back, relax; read a book or have a long bubble bath. You need to pamper yourself, try some self-care as they say." He gave her a quick kiss and then reached for his coat. "I'd better get going. Call me if anything comes up. I'll be home as soon as I can."

She watched him walk out the door, feeling the silence envelope her like a shroud. She picked the plates from the table and set them in the dishwasher. This wasn't fair. This shouldn't be happening to her. The house was perfect...maybe too perfect. She remembered a saying her dad used to always repeat. If it's too good to be true, then it is. Kind of like buying the perfect home for her business and finding that it's haunted. And not with some benign ghost, but with an exasperating being, who loved messing with their heads.

Enough! This moping around feeling sorry for herself wasn't solving the problem. And that was one thing she'd had no time for, languishing in some kind of victimhood. This was a setback to her dream, that was all. She'd somehow convince Liam to move on—for all of their sakes!

She took a deep breath and looked around the kitchen. "I know you're here, Liam. I also know that we talked last night in my dream. You think Ginny is coming back, and that's why you're here. Ginny is dead, Liam. So are you and Rose and Sean. We showed you the soil from your grave. What is it going to take to convince you to leave?"

But if she'd expected any kind of response, she didn't get it. Everything remained still in the house, with only the sound of her own heartbeat pulsing in her ears. Giving her head a shake, she took her purse from the counter and rummaged for James Pratt's email address that he'd given her. Sending him the link to her website was one thing she could accomplish before the electrician showed up.

When she found the small post-it note, she grabbed her cell phone and then went back up to the small office nook. After booting the laptop up she settled in the chair and typed out an email including the website link to send to James. Before she hit the icon to send it, she paused.

After what had happened when Lillian was there, the office getting trashed when they discussed the Pratt family, she wondered if she'd be better off leaving this alone. She could ask Hannah to help with the website on the weekend.

No. Her eyes narrowed, and she tapped the icon to send the email. There. That's that, and 'Mister Gallagher's Ghost' could bloody well lump it! Liam's antics had caused them enough grief. It was time to assert control in this house. She got up and went into the ensuite bath to shower and get ready to face the day.

***

It was almost nine a.m. on the dot when the electrician showed up to check the wiring. Sharon let out a sigh when she saw who was at the door. Damn, she didn't cancel the appointment! She put a smile on her face, opened the door and told him what she needed. He headed to the cellar to look at the circuit panel.

With a fresh peach cobbler in the oven — something to give James Pratt for taking the time to tweak her website—she sat at the kitchen table with her laptop. She was about to open a new tab researching ways to cleanse a house of spiritual entities when her cell phone dinged with a text message. Her eyebrows popped high when she saw that it was Lillian rather than Peter or Hannah.

> **How was your night? I hope things were quiet, and you could get some rest. I hope you don't**

> mind, but I sent an email to the historical society in Brockville on your behalf. I know you're busy and I had some time to spare at the library. (Who am I kidding? It broke the monotony, so thanks for that LOL) They just sent a reply which I printed for you. If you're not busy, I can bring pastries over, if you'll make coffee.

Sharon's head tilted to the side and smiling, she typed her reply.

> Sounds great. Thanks for doing that! I meant to do it but you know... mind like a sieve these days. See you shortly.

She rose to pitch the remnants of the stale coffee and make a fresh pot. When the electrician cleared his throat to get her attention, she almost jumped out of her skin. She set the pot down and turned to him, "All done?"

"Pretty much. I checked the panel, the outlets and I can't see any problems. Everything is not only up to code, but there are many upgrades." His forehead tightened, "I don't see why lights would flicker or there'd be any power surges or interruptions. There're no mechanical issues."

Sharon had totally expected that this would be his finding. She shrugged. "We wanted to make sure and now we are. Thanks for checking everything. If you send me the invoice, I'll look after—"

"Just one thing, though." The portly man scratched his head, staring down at the floor for a moment. "Install some more lights and better heating in the basement. It's damp and chilly down there and a few times I had a hard time finding my testing meter. I'll give you a quote on that work along with the bill."

Sharon was silent for a few beats, watching him. There was no doubt in her mind why it had seemed chilly and why he'd misplaced tools. That was Liam's work no doubt. But there wasn't any point in getting into that with him. "I'll talk to my husband, about that. A few more lights in the basement probably wouldn't hurt."

At the tap on the front door, the man jerked and then looked over at Sharon. It was clear to Sharon that he wasn't at all comfortable being there any longer. She smiled at him. "That's my friend, Lillian." She walked across the kitchen, signaling that she'd see him to the door. He picked up his tool belt and beat a path ahead of her.

Lillian's stepped back to let him go by. "I'm sorry. I should have noticed the truck and that you're busy. I hope I'm not—"

"Nope. Mr. Albertson was just leaving anyway. Come in!" Sharon stepped back and extended her hand, inviting Lillian inside. "I'll be just a moment with the coffee. I can't wait to see what you've learned from that historical society."

Lillian went into the kitchen and took a seat at the table. As she pulled the printed email from her purse, she looked over at Sharon. "They didn't have a lot of info about Liam but apparently there was another son. Patrick was the oldest child. He was killed overseas during the war in 1939."

Sharon's mouth fell open as she finished making the coffee. "Losing a son in the war had to be hard on Liam. He must have been their oldest child. I wonder why there was no mention of him on the gravestone."

"Yes, that's odd, but he was probably buried overseas." Lillian sighed. "There were two sons, one who died in the war, and the other crippled by polio. I wonder what happened to the daughter that she ended up buried in the same plot as her parents. She must not have married."

Sharon grimaced, "It sounds like it. No one to carry on the family name is kind of tragic." When the oven timer dinged, she turned to check the dessert she'd made earlier. A quick peek showed that it needed a few more minutes baking.

"That smells good. What are you baking?" Lillian opened the box of turn-overs. "Maybe I didn't need to bring these."

Sharon smiled at her friend, "It's a peach cobbler for the Pratts. James offered to look at my website for the B&B. Maybe after we have our coffee, we can go for a walk and drop it off to them."

She went still as her body bloomed with heat. Damn. The heat from the oven combined with her own tropical moment made Sharon's cheeks flush. Before she set the mugs of coffee down, she nodded to Lillian. "Let's go out to the sun porch and have this. I feel like some fresh air." Who is she kidding? She wished they had a walk in freezer, not just a sunroom.

Lillian scooped up the box and her purse and followed Sharon down the hallway. "I'd like to meet the Pratts, especially after all that I've learned from Aunt Mary."

When they were settled, Sharon read the email, but it was just as Lillian had said. There was not much more that they didn't already know nothing that would help in getting Liam to leave.

Her eyebrows rose high, recalling the dream she'd had. "I dreamed of Liam last night, Lillian." She paused for a few moments before she continued, "Except I'm not sure if it was real or if it was a dream."

Lillian's head tipped to the side, "What? What do you mean?"

"It was so vivid! I smelled his pipe smoke and heard him comment on the crescent moon before he wandered off. But the really weird thing was that when I got up this morning, there were grass stains and a smudge of dirt on my feet."

Lillian's eyes popped wide, the mug of coffee in her hand pausing before her. "Oh, my god. Are you sure?"

Sharon rolled her eyes before blurting, "Sure the dirt was there or sure I had the dream?"

Lillian flustered, setting the mug down. "That came out wrong, I'm sorry. I believe you, but how could that be? Unless you were sleepwalking. Does that happen to you?"

"No. I mean, I don't remember everything from my childhood, but surely my parents would have told me if I'd ever done that. And definitely, I've never walked in my sleep as an adult. But it's the only thing that makes sense, right?"

"And Peter slept right through it? What did he say when you told him?"

Sharon's shoulders slumped as she sat back in the wicker loveseat. "I didn't tell him about that part of the dream—the dirt and grass stains on my feet. He's worried enough with all of this. Especially when I zoned out sensing Liam and Ginny's presence after my office was trashed."

Lillian edged forward in her chair across from Sharon. "I don't like this, Sharon. Not only is that unsettling, but it's dangerous! What if you'd tripped and hit your head? Who would know? Peter slept right through it."

At the piercing electronic blare, Sharon jerked upright in the loveseat. Her head rose, sniffing the air. Smoke? Oh shit! She jumped to her feet, "The peach cobbler!" With that she raced into the house, her mouth falling open as she saw the cloud of smoke billowing from the kitchen.

Lillian was right behind her. "I'll get the smoke alarm; you get the oven."

Sharon waved her hands, trying to clear a path in the smoke as she hurried to the stove. Opening the oven made her step back when another plume of the burned cake hit her smack in the face.

The room became quiet and Lillian yelled, "Got it! At least we know the smoke alarms work. But we weren't out there that long for the cobbler to burn so bad."

Sharon plopped the blackened dessert onto the stovetop. When she reached to turn the oven off, she blinked a few times to confirm what she saw. Holy cow! The temperature was set on broil!

She snapped the dial back, so that everything was off and then spun around to face Lillian. "He did it again! He jacked up the heat setting all the way up while we were in the sunroom! Oh, my God. What am I going to do?"

Lillian's eyes were round, her gaze pinging between Sharon and the stove. "It was because you were making this for the Pratts! I bet that's why he screwed around with the temperature setting." She shook her head from side to side, "He really has it in for those people."

"And me! Look at all he's done to wreak havoc in this

house. If I could get my hands on that jerk, I'd drown him myself!" Sharon stormed over to the window and pushed the sash wide open. She coughed as the smoke wafted past her, sucked out into the cool air outside.

Lillian stepped over to help fan the room but then grabbed Sharon's arm after a few waves. "Come on! Let's go for that walk right now! It'll give the house a chance to air out. So much for your offering of thanks to the Pratts. That ain't happening."

Sharon's teeth ground together as she glared around the room. "You have to stop this shit, Liam!" She stopped in the doorway, pulling against Lillian's grip. "You don't belong here!"

Lillian grabbed Sharon's jacket from the hook and then darted back into the kitchen to scoop up the cell phone and her purse. "This has to end. You can't keep living like this, Sharon."

Sharon's heart pounded like a jackhammer in her chest. She shoved her arms into the jacket and stomped down the steps to the backyard. "You're right about the Pratts, Lillian. Anytime we talk about them in the house, things get worse. This goes well beyond being a prank. Liam becomes enraged when we even talk about them."

Lillian held the gate open and patted Sharon's shoulder as she strode out. "Why not pick something up at the bakery to bring to them? After all this, I'm really eager to meet them."

"Sure. I won't have Liam dictating what I will or won't do. Besides which, even if the Pratt ancestors were involved in Liam's death, it has nothing to do with James and Sandy!" She stopped short at the next thought, staring at Lillian. "James keeps getting hurt whenever he does something to help speed the renovations along. You don't suppose…?"

"Oh dear. You think that Liam has something to do with that?" Lillian's face was tight as she peered at Sharon. "Is that even possible?" Face palming her forehead, she continued. "Listen to me! Trying to determine the mechanics of a ghost haunting!"

She pulled Sharon's arm, heading down the street to the Pratts. "This is crazy. I vote, get the pastries, meet the Pratts and then go for a long walk. Afterwards, we'll go for lunch and have a drink. I never drink during the day but I think you could use one, Sharon." She laughed lightly. "Who am I kidding? After the peach cobbler episode, *I* need one!"

Sharon was more inclined to have waaay more than just one drink. "I'll second that!" She looked over at Lillian. "I'm glad you stopped by today. Sometimes it feels like I'm losing my mind with all this. It helps that you were there with me when this happened."

"Well, to be honest, I was worried about you. The email from the historical society was a good excuse to check in on you, especially with Peter at work and you home alone. Have you given any thought to getting the minister in to bless the house?" Lillian paused before they entered the bakery, looking at Sharon.

"That isn't an option that we want to pursue. It's just not us, Lillian, although I appreciate your suggestion." Her chest fell, "Peter wants to go with the ghostbuster route. But I'd like to do some research and see what I can come up with. Liam is a total pain, and I'd love to give him a slap right about now, but there's a connection between us. I feel it in my bones."

"Whatever you decide, I'll help you however I can. You know that, right?"

Sharon smiled at her friend. "Careful. I might just take you up on that." She led the way into the store to buy a sweet dessert. Finding out how to banish their resident ghost had been another item on that day's agenda that just got scorched. But it was still relatively early in the day. After a long walk along the shore, she'd tackle that once more.

She had to do something to get some peace in their home. It was that or give up on her dream. Shit. That but it would mean another move. Neither prospect appealed to her.

NINETEEN

Ten minutes later, after the detour to the bakery, Sharon tapped on Pratt's door. She exchanged a nervous glance with Lillian and then forced a smile. When James opened the door, she stammered. "Hi James! I'm sorry for just stopping by unannounced. I hope I'm not interrupting anything."

His eyebrows pulled together, and he shook his head. "No. I was just working on your website."

When he looked over at Lillian, Sharon pressed on. "Lillian, this is James Pratt and James, my friend Lillian Babcock. Lillian works at the library part time." She thrust the bag of pastries into James's hand. "I brought these for you. For helping me with my website."

Lillian interjected. "She had a peach cobbler in the oven, but we got talking and it burned." She looked around at the front of the house and gardens. "Nice place you have here, James. Sharon told me that your grandfather owned this place at one time?

"Yeah, this old place has been in the family for years and years."

Footsteps from the inside of the house were followed by Sandy appearing next to him. She smiled seeing Sharon standing there. "Hi! This is a pleasant surprise. Would you like to come in for a coffee?"

Sharon looked over at Lillian and then introduced the two women. "Thanks, but we don't want to interrupt…"

"Nonsense! You aren't interrupting at all." Sandy reached past James, opening the door wider. "I've been painting the woodwork and I need a break, anyway."

Lillian's nod to Sharon was almost imperceptible, and she added. "I'd love to see what you've done with your home. My aunt knew your grandfather back when he operated a store here."

That remark hit home for James. His face lit up, and he extended his hand, inviting them in. "That's cool. Come in. I'd love to hear more." He gave the bag of pastries to Sandy. "Sharon brought these. But you know I don't mind working on the website; it gives me something productive to do."

As they passed the enormous room on the main floor Sandy paused, lifting the plastic sheeting covering the door opening. "This room is just about done. We're leaning towards making it an art gallery as opposed to a shop. I made a few calls to artists in the area and they're really excited about displaying their art here." Sandy grinned, "With a bit of luck the room will be ready for a reception for the townspeople next weekend. I just have to convince James this is what we need to do."

Sharon caught James's frown at his wife's comment. Pretending not to notice, she inched closer to the doorway to watch the plasterers work on the seams of the new drywall. A gigantic picture window at the back of the room showed a small yard and a dock extending out into the blue water. Her eyebrows bobbed high, "What a beautiful view! This will be a lovely room."

Lillian murmured her agreement, looking around the room. "This room was the original dry goods store your grandfather ran, I'd venture. I'm glad you retained the original hardwood floors. It adds a lot of character."

They followed James and Sandy up the set of stairs to their

private living quarters. Lillian once more remarked. "It looks like your house is coming together quite nicely. It's funny. Aunt Mary remembers your family's store and here I am visiting it just as their descendants are reclaiming it."

Sharon squeezed Lillian's hand, warning her silently to avoid the negative history of the family. When they entered the main living room, Sandy excused herself to get coffee for all of them. James offered with a wave of his hand for them to take a seat on the sofa. He then sat across from them, looking at Lillian.

"I hope your aunt can come to the opening reception. I'd love to chat with her about my family. It was actually my great grandfather who ran the store, so I'm guessing your aunt was very young when she knew them."

Lillian nodded. "Yes, that's true. But wild horses couldn't keep Aunt Mary away from visiting to see the changes." She glanced over at Sharon before remarking, "I wish I had her memory. She remembers the people who once lived in Sharon's home as well—the Gallaghers. Did your parents or grandparents ever mention that family?"

James's head jerked back, and he answered quickly. "No. That name isn't at all familiar. There are times I wish my ancestors had kept a journal. All that history is lost." He peered at Sharon, "And your house has a history with locals as well."

Sharon's heart jumped into her throat and she wished that they'd taken a pass on staying for coffee. She swallowed hard, "Yes. My house has quite a history..." She glanced over at Lillian and murmured softly, "... still does."

Lillian smiled at Sandy when she came in the room with a tray of coffee mugs and the pastries. "I was just telling your husband about the Gallagher's who were an original family in Westport. They owned the home where Sharon now lives." As she took the mug, she continued, "According to Aunt Mary, your family and the Gallagher's weren't the best of friends, James."

Sandy took a seat and grinned. "Oooo. Local gossip and family feuds. I guess every tiny village has its share of that kind of thing."

James sat forward, peering at Lillian. "I wish that my grandparents had told me about that. I wonder what happened between them. Maybe the Gallagher's ran up some bills at the store and couldn't pay. Who knows?"

Sharon jumped in before Lillian said anything more. "Could be. It was during the war and from what I've read, that was a hard time for many families. Liam Gallagher lost a son in that war."

Lillian tsked. "That was before Liam drowned in the lake. He left a crippled son and daughter for his wife to raise. The really odd thing about his death was the timing. He died on Halloween night."

Sandy let out a long sigh. "That's awful. And a little eerie, don't you think? Drowning on Halloween?" She blinked and smiled. "Sounds like something from a Stephen King book. Why on earth would he be out on the water on a night in October?"

As Lillian and Sandy talked, Sharon had zeroed in on James's face. It was clear that he was thinking hard as he listened. When Sandy finished, he looked over at Lillian. "That is tragic. His death was accidental? Did your aunt know anything more?" His voice had a casual edge to it; like some TV detective.

Bingo. Sharon knew that James was fishing with that question. She spoke, having decided that the truth was the best option. "There was suspicion regarding his death. I found an old note in the house about that. It appears to be written by his daughter. She said that her father was a drinker, a gambler and a prankster. She also stated that his drowning was suspicious."

Sandy smiled and took a sip of her coffee. "Oh my God! Not only feuds, but a suspicious drowning! This keeps getting darker by the minute."

Ignoring his wife, James's gaze flitted between Lillian and Sharon. "Are you implying that my family had something to do with this Liam's death? That's preposterous. I hate to cast shade on your aunt, Lillian, but she sounds like she might be a bit batty—no offense."

Oh shit. Sharon saw the flash of anger in her friend's eyes. Cutting Lillian off before she could add fuel to the fire, she decided on a different tack. "It was many years ago, James. I'm afraid none of us really know what happened the night Liam drowned."

Lillian's chin rose high as she flashed a tight smile at James. "My aunt's mind, and my uncle Frank's as well, is perfectly sound; not batty at all." She shot a pointed look at Sharon before continuing. "We haven't told you everything, James. There are some odd things going on in Sharon's home that I've seen with my own eyes."

James snorted, dismissing Lillian. "I'm not sure I want to know about the 'odd' things. I'm hoping it isn't personal, but I'd guess it's just more stories having to do with this Liam character nonsense."

Sandy sat forward in her chair, ignoring her husband's comment. "What kind of odd things, Sharon? Are you saying what I think you're saying?" When James went to say something else, she shushed him with a wave of her hand. "Seriously. I'd like to know. James is a skeptic when it comes to anything paranormal, but I'm not. That's what you're hinting at, isn't it?"

The last thing that Sharon had wanted to discuss with the Pratts was the haunting in her home. But now that Lillian opened that can of worms, what choice did she have? She was certainly not going to dismiss what she'd seen with her own eyes because of James's narrow-minded attitude.

She could feel her cheeks heat when she looked over at Sandy. "Yes. I know how this sounds, believe me, but there are things that have happened without a logical explanation." Seeing Sandy nod, edging even closer on the edge of her seat, Sharon continued. "The TV or music on my cell phone suddenly blares. Even the heat setting in the house has been jacked up with none of us doing that."

James snorted, and then he set his mug on the coffee table with a loud thud. "Have you had it checked by an electrician?

Sounds like a wiring or electrical surge problem to me."

This was not the way Sharon had hoped this would go at all. James's face now had two angry red spots on his cheeks and his eyes had narrowed. Sandy, for her part, looked like a scared rabbit, her gaze flitting between her husband and the women. After all Sharon had been through, having James dismiss this so easily was patronizing.

Keeping her voice even and with a slight smile she answered him, "We have had it inspected twice! No problems at all and the electrical system surpasses the recommended code. There was also an issue with toilet paper being strewn all over my daughter's bath and bedroom in the middle of the night. And before you say it — we don't own a cat or a dog."

James stood up. "Now you're implying that this Liam is haunting your house? And that somehow, my family is mixed up in all that." He shook his head. "Sorry. I don't believe in all this foolishness. Furthermore, I don't like you spreading these stories. I'm trying to establish a life in this village... maybe even open a business."

Sharon stood up. "And I'm not? Why else would I send you that website? Which, please don't spend any more time on. I'll get help from my daughter." She noticed that Lillian had also stood up, but Sharon directed her next remark at Sandy. "You think all the cuts and injuries that James has had doing work here is coincidental? Ask yourself. Has he always been clumsy or accident prone, or did this just happen when he moved here?"

"I'm hardly accident prone. I was almost a professional athlete." James muttered.

Sandy shushed her husband once more. "James renovated our basement in the townhouse we owned in Toronto. All by himself. No injuries and he did a magnificent job."

She stepped by her husband peering at Sharon, "James doesn't believe in anything paranormal, but I do. When I was a teenager, after my parent's divorce, my mother bought a house that was haunted. There was a reason it was cheap and in her price range. I've seen some stuff, let me tell you."

James left the room, and he remarked over his shoulder, "This is total bull. I'm not listening to any more of this ridiculous story."

"It's true, James! I've seen it myself!" Lillian wasn't letting him off the hook that easily.

Sharon turned to Sandy once more. "I'm sorry to lay all this on you. But I'm worried not only about what's going on in my house but what might be at work in yours as well. I hated telling James about his ancestors, but this is real, Sandy. It's pretty scary."

She started walking across the room to the set of stairs. If James was anything like his great grandfather, it was no wonder there was a feud between him and Liam. She couldn't recall the last time she'd met anyone so closed-minded and rigid, not to mention rude, as James. It would be his tough luck if he kept getting injured. She tried.

When they were outside of the house and out of earshot, Sharon turned on Lillian. "Well, that didn't go well at all! Why did you bring that up? You took me by surprise."

Lillian's eyes flew wide open, staring at her. "To get this out in the open! I thought there might be something we could pick up that would help us in getting rid of Liam! I'm sorry it turned out this way." She sniffed before adding, "I guess we won't be getting an invitation to any gallery opening party."

Sharon's gaze shot to Lillian. But then her mouth twitched. The gallery invitation was the least of her worries. "Yeah, I guess we really blew that opportunity for an evening out! How will I ever get over it?" She chuckled. "He was a real jerk, so insufferable and arrogant. Imagine if he had got picked for a major league hockey team. He'd be even harder to be around. I feel sorry for Sandy."

Lillian's chin rose, "Guys like him make being single appealing, that's for sure." As they walked from the sidewalk to the greenbelt along the waterfront, she looked out at the Pratt's dock. "I wonder where Liam drowned. We might be right on the spot where the kids found his body."

Following Lillian's gaze, Sharon scanned the shoreline and

then out to the Pratt's dock. It was missing more than a few boards and had tipped to one side from years of being battered by ice and snow. A shiver gripped her shoulders as she watched the water lap at the thick underlying supports. "We're a month from Halloween and that water looks darned cold already. I think it's safe to say that Liam wasn't out in a boat that night. Especially not on Halloween night."

"Yes, I'd have to agree." Lillian continued walking towards the shore.

Sharon stood still, mesmerized by the choppy waves slapping the dock. When a gust of wind hit her face, she tugged the collar of her jacket higher and folded her arms across her chest. Despite the cool air, she couldn't tear herself away from staring at the dock. A cloud passed over the bright sunshine casting a gloom and turning the water an iron grey shade.

The sounds of seagulls squawking as they swooped and dived faded until there was only silence surrounding her. Her stomach became queasy and a fuzzy vibration rippled through the front of her head. The smell of pipe smoke filled her nose while a shimmering glimmer appeared at the end of the dock. Her mouth fell open when it moved and faded at the farthest point of the wooden platform.

Liam.

She stumbled back, barely catching herself from falling when her heel caught on a stone behind her. Her breath came in a fast pant and her heart pounded quickly. The dullness of the day seemed to thicken and bear down in her, forcing her to sink down on the ground. It became hard to breathe and sadness filled her chest.

This was the spot where Liam had met his end. She could feel the icy chill of the water. The last thing she was aware of was a woman's face worn with worry lines filling her mind's eye before darkness claimed her. Just as everything went dark, she heard Liam's voice in her mind.

'Ginny!'

***

Something gripped her shoulders, lifting and shaking her all at the same time. Her eyes opened slowly, and she blinked a few times until Lillian's face became focused above her.

"Sharon! What's wrong?"

Sharon gulped a lungful of air and grasped her friend's arm, trying to sit up. Lillian's voice sounded like it was coming from inside a rain barrel. She coughed, and it came back to her. She'd sensed Liam's presence at the end of the dock and then his death! And that face she'd seen! It had been Ginny.

"I'm worried, Sharon! You blacked out! Are you all right?" Lillian's eyes were round marbles behind the eyeglasses, peering closely at her.

"Oh my God, Lillian! I... I saw Liam on the dock. He died in the water beside it. I felt the cold and saw his last memory— Ginny's face—before it ended for him." Sharon sat forward and hugged her knees, willing the dizziness from her head. But that sadness she'd felt before blacking out was still there. It was the same feeling she'd had when she'd 'seen' Liam and Ginny in her bedroom the night before.

Lillian rubbed Sharon's back, "We need to get you home. I don't like this. You were fine when I wandered away and then when I turned around you were on your side, lying on the ground. You were totally out of it."

Sharon straightened and turned her head to gape at Lillian. "It came over me so fast. I felt that fuzzy feeling and then I could tell that Liam was here. But not just here, Lillian, but on that dock! He wanted me to know where it happened."

"At the Pratts. This backs up our theory that they had something to do with his death!" She looked over at the Pratt's house. "Not Sandy or that jack-ass James, of course... but his grandfather!" She hooked her hands in the crook of Sharon's arm and helped her up.

Sharon took a few deep breaths before she let Lillian help her walk back from the shore to the sidewalk. When her foot hit the cement, she felt steady enough to shrug Lillian's hand from her arm. "I'm okay, now. But I really could use that drink. It wasn't bad enough with Liam ruining the dessert and then the argument with James, but then this blackout thing happens to me..."

Lillian looked over at her. "You might want to make that drink a strong cup of tea. That was scary, Sharon. Have you ever blacked out before when you've had these spells?"

Sharon trudged slowly up the street, grateful that her house wasn't far away. This had never happened to her, even as a child when these 'vision spells' were more common. "I've never blacked out, Lillian. This is getting worse."

At the next thought, she gripped Lillian's wrist. "Please don't tell Peter about this! You can tell him about all the rest, but not that I blacked out. He'll have me going to the doctor for God knows how many CAT scans and tests." She grimaced. "Probably a head-shrinker too."

Lillian's eyes narrowed as she gaped at Sharon. "No. He has to know about this. He's your husband! I have to tell him. If anything more happened and you were seriously injured or became sick, I'd—"

"Fine! But don't embellish it. I slipped into unconsciousness for a few moments. I feel fine now, although I am having something stronger than tea when I get home. I think I've earned that." Her eyes closed for a moment as she thought about what Peter would say. Shit. She could just see it now. He'd be worried, coddling and restricting her movements when apparently this was transitory. If it wasn't for Liam and going through the change of life she'd be right as rain.

"Have a stiff drink or two but I'm making you lunch! I think you need to rest, maybe take a nap this afternoon. It's a good thing I don't have to work today. I'll stay with you until Peter gets home." Lillian's chin rose, and she stared down her nose at Sharon, defying her to challenge that decision.

Sharon sighed even though inside she was glad that Lillian would keep her company. The last thing she needed that day was being alone when there was the chance that Liam would pull another prank.

TWENTY

An hour later with two shots of Jack Daniels in her belly, along with tomato soup and some crackers, Sharon felt a lot less jittery. While Lillian was busy loading the dishwasher, Sharon opened her laptop to search for information regarding cleansing a home of ghosts. It had been something she'd planned on doing that day and now after that 'spell' it seemed even more important.

When she'd looked before after acknowledging that her house was haunted, there'd been pages of sites to help. But this time she needed something more useful than just asking Liam to move on, or commanding him to stop with his tricks. Many articles mentioned using a sage smudge to cleanse the house from top to bottom.

Lillian pulled out the chair to sit beside her. "What are you doing? Anything I can help with?"

Sharon adjusted the screen so they both could read it. "I'm looking for cleansing rituals to finish this thing with Liam." She touched the screen at a site that looked legitimate. "Let's try this one." She looked over at Lillian, "They all recommend smudging your home with sage to get rid of unwanted spirits.

There's got to be something to that."

"Smudging is something that's popular with Indigenous people. I've read a little about it, getting rid of negative energy. Sage, sweetgrass and cedar are popular." When Sharon shot a curious look at her, Lillian shrugged. "It's not that busy at the library and I get tired of playing Free Cell. I'm a walking encyclopedia of useless trivia."

"Maybe not so useless, Lillian." Sharon started reading the page when it loaded. 'Be sure to open a door or window so that the entity has a way to leave. Chant a phrase like 'Go in peace. Whatever ties that you feel keep you here don't matter. You must leave this plane of existence.'

Lillian murmured, "That sounds straightforward enough. As for the bundle of sage, I'm sure we can pick up supplies at the Reservation in Deseronto. It's only an hour away."

Sharon sat back and looked at her friend. "So you want to help me with this? Are you sure?"

"Are you kidding me? I wouldn't miss it for all the world." Lillian fixed her with a stern look, "You blacked out earlier, Sharon. Do you think I'd let you do this alone? I'm not sure how Peter will feel about all this though. He may have a point about getting a professional in to do this."

Sharon's gaze fell to the table. Lillian had a point about Peter. Especially when he found out that she'd passed out for a few minutes. This might be a hard sell to get him to agree with tackling this on their own. She looked over at Lillian, "We may end up having to get a professional but not before I give this a try."

She sighed, "There's some kind of connection between Liam and me. He's shown himself to me and he's pointing out what led to his death. Getting a stranger in would make matters worse."

"Well, one thing is clear to me..." Lillian looked around the room as she spoke, "Having nothing more to do with the Pratts has got to help. For what it's worth, Liam, James Pratt is a jerk."

Sharon's gaze flitted over to the stove, the site of Liam's

latest prank. But there was nothing, no shimmering or odd feeling that he was even in the room with them. But there'd been many instances of calm before Liam pulled a stunt.

"Would you like to go tomorrow to pick up the sage? If we go in the morning, we can be back to do the smudging in the afternoon. Or are you working?" Sharon went back to the article on-line, clicking it closed.

"No, I'm free tomorrow until five when I have to help Aunt Mary set up for her card game evening with her cronies." Lillian peered closely at Sharon, "You look tired. Why don't you lay down for a bit. I'll stay and read my novel."

A nap sounded like a great idea. Whether it was the two shots of the whiskey or a result of that encounter at the waterfront, Sharon felt bone weary. It was a little after three and Peter wouldn't be home until five or six, so she had time. Besides, looking rested and fresh when Lillian ratted her out to Peter would help her case.

***

When Sharon woke from a dreamless sleep, the dim light in the room was disorienting. Holy Hannah! What time was it? A glance at the bedside clock showed that it was almost seven in the evening! She'd slept for four hours? She had been more tired than she'd thought, for her to sleep that long during the day. That episode at the waterfront had taken a lot out of her.

Throwing the comforter aside, she stretched, and then slowly got out of bed. For whatever reason, her muscles felt like she'd run a marathon. It was definitely not the fresh, perky side she'd wanted to show Peter. When she trudged down the steps, she heard him in the kitchen, before she smelled the pizza he'd brought home.

Standing at the kitchen sink, Peter turned when she entered. "How are you feeling? Before she left, Lillian told me about what happened today." The look he shot at Sharon showed more worry than anything else. "I don't like the fact that you blacked out, Sharon."

She took a seat at the table and forced a smile. "Honestly, I'm fine now. I'm sure it sounds worse than it actually was. It was only for a minute or two, but at least I know where Liam drowned."

"Fat lot of good that will do for us. I'm more worried about you, Shar! I wish we'd never bought this place." Peter came over and took a seat across from her, reaching to place his hand on hers. "It's not worth your health or what we've gone through since we've been here."

Sharon's heart sunk into her stomach. There was no way she wanted to give up on the house. Peter was understandably upset, but that didn't mean they should give up. If anything, she was getting closer to solving the problem with Liam's death and why he kept hanging around.

Before she could argue the point, Peter kept going. "I called the former owner today. I figured that you might not think of it and besides, I wanted to give her a piece of my mind, if she knew about the weird things that are happening in this house and didn't tell us."

Sharon leaned closer, her curiosity winning over any feeling of uneasiness that she'd forgotten to make that phone call. But it seemed like these days, she forgot a lot of things. "What'd she say?"

Peter's eyebrows arched, and he shook his head. "You think the conversation with the Pratts was tense? I'm sure it was nothing to the earful I got from Bonnie! She told me that nothing 'odd' had ever happened when she and her husband lived here, aside from him taking up with another woman. She thought we were trying to set up some kind of case to sue her or something for misrepresentation. She made it sound like we were scam artists."

Sharon's eyes narrowed, "Really? No music blaring or lights flickering when she lived here?" When Peter shook his head, she squeezed his hand, "See? If we believe her, then all this weird, ghostly stuff only happened when we moved here. I knew it! It's because of *me*... and maybe because of the Pratts suddenly moving back to the village."

"Which means we're right back to where we started, no further ahead in getting Liam to leave." His mouth was a tight line when he added, "Lillian told me about you two planning on doing some ritualistic smudging to get him to leave. I'm not in favor of that, Sharon, not after what happened to you today. Why not call in a medium or shaman or whatever name they go by?"

Sharon got up and opened the oven to get her pizza. All the while her mind raced to find a good counterargument. She didn't know why exactly, but she felt all the way down to her bones that bringing in someone new would make matters worse. She slid into her seat at the table with her plate.

"Not yet. Let me do the smudging thing with Lillian tomorrow and then we'll talk about a medium. I'm not willing to give up, Peter. Believe me, I'm as eager as you are to put an end to Liam's presence in this house. But I'd rather do it on my own terms."

Peter sat back and folded his arms across his chest. "I'd rather have my wife safe than anything else. If you're insistent on doing this tomorrow, then I insist that I be here. If you have another of these spells, then it all stops. That's my condition. Agreed?"

Sharon hid the relief she felt that he hadn't completely shot down her plan. Especially after the fainting spell. She was lucky he hadn't pushed her to go to the doctor. Yet, anyway.

She nodded, letting a hint of exasperation flavor her tone when she spoke. "Fine. We're in this together. Lillian and I had planned on doing the smudging in the afternoon. Can you get away from work, because I don't want to put this off. Hannah will be home on the weekend and I'd really like to have this settled before she has to go through any of this again."

Peter let out a fast huff. "Think I don't want it finished? But more importantly, I want you healthy and well."

He snitched a pepperoni from the slice of pizza on her plate and popped it into his mouth. "I was talking to Ike Nickerson about James Pratt and hockey. Ike's a die-hard Toronto fan even though the Leafs never amount to anything. Hope springs eternal and all that. He knew about James Pratt being scouted."

Sharon gaped at him. "What? He's some kind of super-fan if he follows draft picks and all that stuff. Was he impressed that James is our neighbor?" She murmured under her breath, "Although he wouldn't be if he ever met James, that nasty prick."

Peter snorted. "Your friend Lillian doesn't think much of James either. While you were napping, she told me about you meeting the guy. Arrogant and narrow-minded was how she described him." Peter's smile fell when he continued. "But what Ike told me about James' time as a hockey pro is a little weird."

"Oh?" Sharon perked up. "What about it?"

"Apparently there was another player who everyone thought was a sure bet. Elliott Walsh. They brought him up from Nova Scotia for the try-outs, thinking he'd be another Wayne Gretzky. But during a practice scrimmage, he went head-first into the boards and fractured his skull." Peter shook his head. "That was the end of his career."

"That's a shame. I wonder if James knew him. It's such a dangerous sport. I'm glad our son never went beyond house league."

Peter got up and took Sharon's empty plate to the dishwasher. "According to Ike, they were both there during the pre-season training camp last year. I'd bet James knew him. But after your visit with the Pratts today, I doubt whether we'll ever get the opportunity to ask him."

"Small loss in my opinion... except for Sandy. I feel sorry for her. I hope I didn't make her life more stressful. I think that things between them are tense enough as it is. She sided with Lillian and me when I told them about some of the creepy things happening here."

"I wish that you and Lillian hadn't got into that with them. It's not that I thought we could be great friends or anything, but I hate that word might get around the village about our house. Not everyone is as open-minded as Lillian. A lot of people would think we're crazy." Peter stepped behind Sharon and rubbed her shoulders. "How about we set all this aside and just watch a movie tonight? I think you need a mental escape after the day that you had."

Sharon reached and patted Peter's hand. "That sounds good. You get it set up and I'll make some popcorn. We could both use a break from this."

When he left the room Sharon rose from her chair. As she set making their snack, her thoughts were like the tail of a kite, bouncing helter-skelter over what had happened that day as well as the conversation with Peter. There was something niggling in the back of her mind— something that didn't quite fit with what the Pratts' had said.

They'd come to Westport to establish a life here, totally caught up with renovating the house to the point that James was rushing the project. But why was that? They didn't seem to have any concrete plan of what they were going to do once the house was done, especially with that downstairs room. They'd mentioned making it a tea room or art gallery. But wouldn't you know what kind of business to run *before* you renovated that room? When she and Peter had bought this house, there'd been a definite plan in mind—to run a B&B. James and Sandy sounded like they were flailing around in their plans.

She sighed as she shook the pot, coating the kernels with butter. James had definitely over-reacted when she'd told them about the family feud and Liam's death. It wasn't like she was accusing him! Every family had skeletons in their closet. When she'd learned that her own great grandfather and his brother had been rum runners during prohibition, staying just one step ahead of the law, it had been a shock at first but then she'd come to understand. It was another time and things were different. It didn't make Sharon a crook or even complicit just because this was in her family tree.

As Sharon stood at the stove ruminating over the day, she didn't notice the basement door slowly open. The cacophony inside the pot masked the floor creaking behind her. It was only when she felt the air change, cooler on her shoulders that she stiffened, jerked out of her thoughts. Her head felt that same dizzy, fuzzy, tingly feeling before she spun around quickly.

For just a fraction of a second she saw a shadow in the open doorway leading to the downstairs. The smell of cherry tobacco drifted in the air. Liam was there with her in the room. Her heart thundered against her ribcage and she took a deep breath to remain calm. "I know you're here, Liam."

Not for long if all went well tomorrow with the smudging ceremony she planned. She turned back to finish getting the popcorn from the pot. At least he hadn't startled her like he normally did. This time had been just a gentle nudge reminding her he was around.

Her eyes flew open wide. What was he trying to communicate? Was he acknowledging her sympathy when she'd found the site of his death? Or was he giving her some sort of a spectral pat on the back for her taking on James Pratt?

Keeping her eyes on her cooking, she said aloud, "What are you trying to tell me, Liam?" But the aroma of pipe smoke had dissipated. Glancing over at the door to the basement, she saw it was once again closed.

Liam had gone silent.

TWENTY-ONE

It was almost ten the next morning when Lillian joined them to drive to the native reservation to get the smudging supplies. Loaded with a paper tray of coffee and a bag of doughnuts, she tapped on the sunroom door.

Peter tossed the dish towel onto the counter and crossed the kitchen floor. "She's early. I got this, Shar!"

Sharon smiled as she stood before the vanity mirror in the downstairs bathroom putting lipstick on. She called out to Peter, "She needs to be back for something her aunt has going on later this afternoon." She added, "Plus, knowing Lillian, she really wants to be part of the smudging, so she wants to get the show on the road." She set the lipstick down and was just leaving the bathroom when there were another series of raps, but this time at the front door.

Rolling her eyes, she went to go answer it, muttering. "What now? It doesn't rain, but it pours." Her eyebrow rose high seeing Sandy Pratt standing on her front verandah. Unlike her usual smile, Sandy's face was drawn as she hugged her arms across her chest.

Sharon opened the door, "Sandy? Is something wrong? Is it

133

James? Did he get injured again?" Seeing Sandy's frown, she would bet anything she was here because of something to do with James being a total jerk.

She beckoned Sandy in, watching her closely when Sandy blurted out, fighting tears. "We just had an argument! It was almost the biggest fight we've ever had since we've been married! I'm sorry Sharon, but I didn't know who else to turn to."

Sharon patted Sandy's shoulder. "That's okay." When Sandy looked away for a moment, Sharon continued, "It's about Lillian and me visiting yesterday, isn't it? I knew I upset him, but how—"

"You don't know James! He can't take criticism at all. Even when people try to joke around with him... just teasing for laughs, he takes offense."

"I wasn't teasing him, Sandy. For crying out loud, I wasn't even criticizing him! I was just talking about what might have happened between the Pratts and Gallagher's!" She put a hand on Sandy's shoulder. "Did he think I was criticizing him? Because I wasn't, you know."

"I know! I'm trying to figure out what the hell just happened between the two of us just now!" She pursed her lips, thinking. "I've seen him blow his top when people tease him. But this morning... he was just so damn irritable."

When Peter and Lillian stepped into the living room, Sharon shot them a look. "Sandy stopped by for a visit. Can you give us a few minutes here?"

Peter nodded and then ushered Lillian through the archway, going back to the kitchen. Sandy noticed and then swiped at her eyes, brushing away the tears that had welled there. "I'm sorry to just bust in on you. It looks like you're busy. I'll leave—"

Sharon gave Sandy a slight shake to get her attention. "No. You'll sit down and tell me what is going on; I think you need to get something off your chest." She nodded thoughtfully. "It might make you feel better. Peter and Lillian will wait. We have an errand to run but it's not that urgent." It was pretty urgent, with Hannah coming home for the weekend… but poor Sandy was a wreck.

Sandy let Sharon lead her to the sofa and then sunk down into its cushion. "James was really upset with you guys talking about his family. He thinks there will be stories going round about his great grandfather because of what you talked about." Her eyes widened. "Then he started rambling on about what you said about ghosts…" She closed her eyes, a tear appearing at each corner. "When he got on that subject… he went crazy! He said that I was in cahoots with you!"

"What?"

She nodded. "Yes, he lost his grip and was stomping all around saying that I was 'in league with those damn Gallaghers!'"

Sharon went very still. All the air went out of her chest. "Sandy… the Gallaghers are all dead," she said quietly.

"I know!" Her eyes were wild with fear, and Sandy reached for her and held her. She wasn't very much older than her own son Spencer.

There's something to what he said', ran through her head as she comforted the younger woman. Whatever it was, she had no idea; but what Sandy just told her made sense somehow. It just had the ambience of being right.

Sandy pulled away from Sharon's hug for a moment. With her eyes closed and her voice barely audible, she continued, "This was supposed to be a fresh start for us. He was never happy working for the insurance company, even though he was pretty good at it. After he failed at the hockey try-out, he changed. It wasn't just that he was disappointed, he became bitter."

"That had to be difficult for you, Sandy, trying to be supportive and keep his morale up." Sharon had dealt with people going through depression and it took a toll on the family. For someone as cheerful and upbeat as Sandy was, that would be quite challenging.

"It was *impossible*! Don't get me wrong. I love James, but often I had to walk on eggshells around him. And this move!

Everything happened so fast. One day we're hanging in there and the next we're packing up to come here. But at that point, I was willing to try anything to get him back to the way he was when we were first married."

Sharon nodded, but all the while it reaffirmed what she'd thought the night before. It explained why they were so wishy-washy on whatever business they'd set up. They hadn't had time to fully figure anything out before James had made this decision to move to Westport.

Sandy forced a smile when she looked at Sharon. "I'm sorry to dump all this on you. I hardly know you. But at least I feel a bit better getting this off my chest. I should let you get back to whatever it was you were doing."

"That's no problem at all, Sandy. I know we don't know each other, but I liked you right from the start. I just hate to see you going through this. But things will get better. Every marriage has its ups and downs. As long as you love each other, things will even out again." It was a weak platitude, but at the moment, it was the best she could come up with.

A part of Sharon also was conscious of the fact that this was a Pratt in Liam's house, even if she was only a Pratt by marriage. What havoc would Liam wreck after having Sandy there? So when Sandy stood up, ending the visit, Sharon wasn't going to argue the point. Maybe after Liam was convinced to move on, there'd be other times that Sandy would stay longer for a visit. But now wasn't an ideal time.

"Thanks for listening. I hope you're right that things will get better. But I needed a shoulder to cry on." While Sandy spoke she eased away, going towards the front door.

On impulse, Sharon gave Sandy a hug. "Anytime you need to talk, I'm here. I'll call you later if you'd like. Give me your cell number." Sharon fished her phone from her pocket and plugged in the numbers that Sandy dictated.

When she closed the door and turned to go back into the kitchen, she startled in surprise. Peter and Lillian hovered there, waiting for her to speak. She smiled despite herself, seeing the two nosy parkers. "What? She and James had an argument. She was upset."

Lillian's chin rose, "It was about our visit yesterday, wasn't it? He was angry with us and took it out on her. What a jerk!"

Sharon couldn't argue the point. Instead she offered, "It's been hard for Sandy even before we brought up all that stuff yesterday. When he didn't make the team, she said that he was almost impossible for her to live with. And then right out of the blue, he uproots them to move here."

Peter grabbed his car keys from the hook and motioned for them to get going. "From what you're saying, James really rules the roost. He must have some kind of ego to pull that off."

As she followed Peter and Lillian out of the house, Sharon added, "You aren't wrong about that. Sandy said that he gets offended easily, especially when he thinks people are making fun at his expense."

When Peter paused to lock the door behind them, his forehead was knotted looking at Sharon. "I remember playing hockey as a teen in house league. It could get rough being with the other players, and I don't mean taking a hip check or being bounced into the boards. You need a real thick skin to lace up your skates and take shots. Everyone rides everyone's ass, all the time."

Lillian interrupted, "You mean teasing don't you? Hockey metaphors are lost on me, I'm afraid. Not a fan."

"Sure. That's kind of a male thing, I guess. It's not just hockey, Lillian. Guys will tease the hell out of you, but they usually don't mean anything by it. It's just communication." Peter shrugged. "I don't make the rules. It's just the way it goes. That sure must have been hard on someone lacking a sense of humor, like James."

***

It was just after lunch when they returned from the trip to the Mohawk reservation. Sharon entered the house and her eyes did a quick recognizance of things in the family room. The cushions on the sofa were as they had left them and the air in the room was just slightly warmer than outside — so no one had monkey'd with the heat setting.

Behind her, Peter murmured, "I can't believe I'm actually going to do this. Despite what that lady in the Wildfeather store said, that lots of people routinely smudge their homes, it still seems like some kind of hoo-doo thing."

"Are you kidding? This is going to be awesome." Lillian shrugged out of her jacket and rubbed her hands together. "Where shall we start?"

Sharon didn't share Lillian's enthusiasm or Peter's grudging acceptance. Instead, there was a sinking feeling in the pit of her stomach. Although this was necessary, it was also a bit sad. She thought of the note that had been left by Liam's daughter, who had hoped to shed light on her father's death. Well, it had worked.

Sharon had no doubt whatsoever that the Pratts had something to do with Liam's death, but that wasn't the whole reason that he lingered on in the house. His love for his wife and family were also strong ties to the home, which the smudging was about to break.

She hoped.

But this had to end. She took a deep breath and led the way into the kitchen. "Peter, why don't you open all the windows while Lillian and I get the smudging stuff set up? I think we should start in the basement, but those windows are painted shut. We'll leave the door to the kitchen open and hope for the best."

Lillian took the bundle of sweet grass from the bag and looked over at Sharon, "We're going to wait for Peter to join us before we start, right?"

From the wide-eyed look on Lillian's face, Sharon could see that despite her friend's earlier enthusiasm, she was on edge now that they were getting down to business. "Yes, I think we should all be together when we do this."

"Yes, like a triumvirate, the power of three. Just like in church, the holy trinity—"

"Or the three musketeers." Sharon smiled before Lillian corrected her.

"I think there were four of them. Hell! Listen to us. We've

got to get our heads into this. What are you going to say? Have you thought about that?"

Before Sharon had a chance to answer, Peter's shout from upstairs interrupted.

"Sharon! Don't answer the door! I'll be right down."

Lillian's face showed that she was as confused as Sharon. The next thing the two of them heard were Peter's feet thumping fast down the stairs. Sharon rushed to the dining room just as Peter raced across the room and opened the door.

She saw James Pratt striding across the verandah, practically yelling, "Stay away from my family! It wasn't bad enough that your wife and her friend busted into my home yesterday, but now they've got Sandy and other people in the village plotting against me!"

"What the hell are you talking about?"

Sharon heard the anger in Peter's voice, but it was no match for the rage that flooded through her body. She was hardly aware that she almost knocked Peter into the doorjamb when she stomped out onto the wooden platform. She glared at the young man, as if seeing him for the first time. His eyes were chips of granite, while two red spots of fury flared on his cheeks. Yet, he took a step back when she edged even closer.

"What is wrong with you? We tried to help you—"

"Stay away from my wife! Leave us alone or so help me..." His teeth clicked, while the muscle in his jaw tight quivered. At his side, his fingers splayed and then formed fists while his eyes were murderous with pent-up fury.

Sharon's vision blurred, and a wave of dizziness washed through her. Time slowed to a stand-still while the only sound she heard was James's breathing, sounding like the hiss of a cat. She struggled to catch her breath while her body became numb. James's face wavered like heat waves above hot asphalt. The eyes were the same, but a shadow of a mustache appeared and then just as quickly was gone. Her knees buckled, and she began to slip to the floor.

Sharon felt Peter's arm around her shoulders, pulling her upright as her knees turned to water. Her voice sounded strange like it was coming from the end of a long tunnel when she spoke. *"Ye'll kill me? It wouldn't be the first death at a crooked Pratt's hand!"*

Sharon blinked and felt Lillian gripping her arm on the other side. Peter's words, shouting at James Pratt, to get off the property barely registered as *'ye'll kill me?'* pounded like a pulse in her head. Where had that come from? And the rest of it? *'...the first death at a crooked Pratt's hand!'*

She was losing her mind.

Her gaze rose from the floorboards as if pulled by a magnet. Across the road, peering at her like a hawk eying a field mouse, was the old lady. Her gnarled hands clutched the grips of her walker as she stood, meeting Sharon's gaze. Sharon couldn't look away from the old woman even when Peter's arm went around her, trying to steer her back into the house.

"Wait!" Sharon shrugged away from her husband and Lillian. She watched the old lady beckon to her to come over.

Peter stepped closer to Sharon, "What the heck?"

Lillian murmured, "That horrible man. How dare he…" Her words faded when she noticed Peter and Sharon staring at the old woman across the street from them. "Why is Eve Smith waving you over? Do you know her?"

Peter's voice was barely above a whisper, "No. We've seen her scowling at us from her perch over there. She never acknowledges us when we wave to her, so we thought she was senile. She obviously caught the scene with James. What does she want?"

Sharon crossed the verandah and was about to go down the few steps to go talk to the old woman when she felt Peter grip her hand. "I really think this can wait, Shar. After that blow-up with James, we all need to just sit down and cool off. Why did you say 'ye'll kill me' to him? That was weird, and it didn't help matters."

Lillian added, "He deserved it. Are you all right, Sharon? My heart's still going like a race-horse because of that asshole!"

But Sharon continued walking over to the old woman's house, ignoring the two of them. The elderly crone stood riveted to the spot, her gaze never wavering from Sharon's. When she walked up the few stairs, she paused, waiting for the old woman to speak.

It seemed to take forever, but finally Eve Smith nodded. "It's come full circle then, hasn't it." But it wasn't a question. Not from the slight smile on her thin lips as she sank back into her chair.

"What's come full circle? You saw the argument at our house. What do you know about all this?" Sharon didn't wait to be invited to sit down. She grabbed a chair from down the verandah and sat facing the woman. Lillian and Peter stayed on the stairs watching the old woman.

The woman who Sharon had seen a few times going in and out of Eve Smith's house—her caretaker?—stood next to the old woman, adding her two cents. "That was quite a spectacle. You're both newcomers, yet you're already on the outs with each other."

Eve shot a pointed look up at the younger woman. "Would you get me a drink of water, Hilda?" The younger woman's cheeks flushed, but her mouth was a straight line when she left to go into the house.

Eve shook her head as she looked down at her lap. "She means well but sometimes…"

Sharon was doing her best to hold her tongue, but curiosity got the best of her. "What do you know of all this, Mrs. Smith? You know something or you wouldn't have said that we've come full circle."

The old woman nodded. "I've just seen a ghost, my dear."

1943

Liam Gallagher

TWENTY-TWO

It was a scorcher of a day for the last week of September. Liam swiped the beads of sweat from his forehead and then reached for the jug of water. As he chugged a long mouthful, he gazed at the beams of sunshine dancing through the canopy of green above him. Days like this, being out in the fresh air enjoying nature's kaleidoscope of color were always bittersweet—the freedom and beauty were a poignant reminder of days long ago when he'd owned the farm. But the war and the grim time of the Great Depression put an end to that, not to mention the loss of his eldest son, Patrick.

"Just a few more logs ought to do it, Da." Sean extended his hand, signaling for his father to share the bottle.

"Aye." Liam handed the water to Sean. "T'is a good day's haul, I'm thinking. And the horses won't complain about getting back to O'Brien's barn after this." But as he smiled at his son, it wasn't the horses that were his first concern. The boy tried to help as best he could but it was hard to get around with that bum leg, not to mention he tired easily. Ginny worried about their son going to the woodlot to help cut, but she'd been outnumbered when Sean eagerly pushed the issue.

The bloody polio was a nuisance, not a life sentence of confinement.

The last couple of logs, straight and stripped of branches, lay in the grassy glen behind the wagon. As Liam rounded the wagon he looked up at his son, perched on the seat behind the two draft horses. "Back 'er up a few feet, Sean."

When the wagon was in position Liam hefted the biggest log onto the lip of the wagon and manhandled it until it lay next to the others. It was hard work, but it was honest work, and the money came in handy, not to mention the fact that it kept many families from freezing come wintertime.

Ten minutes later, he took a seat next to his son on the wagon. "Think you can handle getting us home in one piece? We've got only two stops and then you're done for the day." He glanced over at his son, his smile hiding the concern when he noticed Sean's grip on the rein falter. But rather than make an issue out of his son being tired from the day's work, he kept up a nonchalant monologue.

"What do you suppose your ma's made for supper, boy? My mouth is watering for a taste of stew with dumplings and apple pie smothered in ice cream for dessert." Liam fished his pipe from the pocket of his shirt and stuffed some tobacco into the bowl.

"Not sure about the ice cream. Rose went to the store for Ma yesterday and old man Pratt said they were out." His son's grey eyes narrowed when he looked over at his father. "Funny thing though is that he had ice cream for his own kids. Rose saw Willie and Maribel Pratt later on with cones stuck in their gobs."

Liam's jaw tightened, clamping the stem of the pipe between his teeth. Leave it to William Pratt to be stingy when it came to anything to do with a Gallagher. If there were any other store in the village, he'd gladly shop there instead. Hell! Practically the entire village felt the same way about the crooked Pratts.

He blew out a plume of cherry smelling smoke and patted his son's good leg. "That's all right, boyo! Your ma's pie is so good, it doesn't need anything more." He couldn't help the added comment that flipped from his lips. "Young Willie's face doesn't need more sweets. The last time I saw him, there were more than a few volcanoes on his fat cheeks ready to erupt. He's a regular Mount Vesuvius."

Sean's lips drew back, "Yuck." But then he laughed. "Mount Vesuvius. That's a good one, Da. Where is that?"

"Italy. It erupted and destroyed Rome way back in the day." Too bad young Willie's face wouldn't erupt all over William Pratt. But he didn't say this out loud. Things were bad enough without adding fuel to the fire.

They continued on for the five miles from the stand of trees to the village, waving impatient automobiles to pass by them. Their first stop was the Smith family on the outskirts of the village. Alf Smith and his wife were a fine couple with a brood of youngsters who were the terror of the new schoolteacher. He didn't know how many times he'd seen a Smith child held after school, writing lines on the chalkboard for punishment. It had always been hard to keep a grin off his face as he went about emptying the trash and mopping the floors.

When they pulled into the drive, Alf emerged from the front door of his two-story clapboard house. "Hi Liam, Sean. Great day for cuttin' wood!" He pushed the sleeves of his shirt higher and called for his two oldest boys to help unload.

Liam hopped down from the wagon and watched the Smith boys climb down from the tree on the edge of the property. "They're getting so big, Alf. I'm glad this war is just about over and they'll miss getting called up."

Alf nodded. "You and me both." He grabbed a log as big round as his thigh and pulled it from the pile, waiting for Liam and the boys to help lift it and set it on the ground. "How're Ginny and Rose?"

Liam smiled, "They're fine. And your missus?" He watched Alf's oldest boy, a fourteen-year-old strapping lad, try to haul a log from the top of the pile. He just about had it, but it got caught on a knot of another log. "Careful lad. If that rolls, you want to watch your fingers."

The red-haired boy's face flushed, but he selected another log to try his hand at. Trying his best to act casual, the boy looked up at Sean, "Are you and Rose going to the Halloween party at the school? It sounds like it will be fun."

Sean smirked, "What you really want to know is if Rose is going. She and Eve talked about it. I'll tell her you were asking, Robbie."

Liam couldn't help the chortle that escaped when he saw the shocked look on the Smith lad's face. Sean might be handicapped physically, but there was no shortage of wit between his ears. But it was all in good fun. Sean wouldn't say anything to Rose that she didn't already know.

When they finished unloading the last of the Smith's logs, Alf looked down at the ground before he spoke to Liam. "Can I pay you for this next month? It's a tad tight with bills right now."

"Of course! Pay me when you can, Alf. We're neighbors. I understand how it is with a growing family." Liam clapped the younger man on the back and leaned in, speaking softly. "Who knows? The way your boy feels about my Rose, maybe we'll share grandchildren someday."

Alf laughed, "I remember those days, courting Irene. The poor lad's got it bad and who could blame him? She's a fine looking gal, your Rose."

Liam nodded and then hauled himself back up onto the wagon. His chest swelled with pride thinking about his children. He and Ginny were blessed all right. If only... But he shut that line of thinking down. His oldest son was gone, and he'd better appreciate the treasures he had.

***

It was later that night when Liam wandered outside to smoke his pipe after Ginny's fine supper. He heard the screen door bang and knew that Rose had decided to join him in the garden. It was their special time together, when the moon had risen and all was still.

When she stepped close to where he leaned over the fence,

he gave her a sidelong glance. "You helped your mother with cleaning up, I gather?"

"Dad! You ask me that every night. Of course. She's knitting in the front room while Sean is reading, as usual." She sidled closer and her voice took on a conspiratorial note. "Have you thought about Halloween? I think the prank with the outhouses is a little passé, don't you? What trick are you thinking of pulling on old Pratt? I'll help."

He puffed on his pipe and nudged her with his elbow. "There are a few young fellas who might miss you at that Halloween party, if you do."

"You mean Robbie Smith? I know he likes me, but Eve's got her cap set on him. Besides, I'd rather be with you, especially if it's a good trick on the Pratts." She was quiet for a few moments and Liam let her stew. There was something on her mind that she'd have to spill sooner or later.

Finally she blurted, "You know that fancy boat they got this summer? Wouldn't it be swell if it got a hole in it and sank. That would show them after them gallivanting all over the lake showing off."

Much as Liam enjoyed the scene that played in his mind with William Pratt crying about his prized motor boat, he shook his head. "No, lass. That would be too much. Halloween's meant to be fun, not dangerous or doing something that would cause such a loss of money. Even the Pratts don't deserve that."

Rose's eyes narrowed when she looked up at him, "They do so deserve it! When I was in the store the other day, you should have heard the way they talked to Mrs. Bennett. They went on and on about her bill, how it's getting so big and they haven't had a payment from her in over a month. Honestly, Da. The poor widow was almost in tears, especially when there were a few other people in the store who heard everything! And then they claimed they were out of ice cream when I asked."

Liam could feel the back of his neck get tighter and tighter as Rose spoke. Mrs. Bennett had lost her husband to cancer the previous year. She'd tried to make ends meet since then, cleaning house for the families who could afford it and there were precious few of them. Her oldest son had moved to Kingston and had a family of his own. He did his best to help her out when he could, but had his own two daughters in school to feed. Times were tough all over and it wasn't like the Pratts were hard up for the money. If they could afford an expensive motor boat and their fancy trip to Toronto at Christmas, Mrs. Bennett's bill wouldn't put them in the poorhouse.

Greed. That was what the Pratts were made of. And enough pride to fill a softball field; not afraid at all to show off their money to a village in hard times. It was tempting to put a hole in that new motor boat. But if Ginny ever found out, she'd kill him. That is, if Pratt's cousin, the copper, didn't get him first.

He smiled at Rose, "Let me give this some thought, darlin'. You're right about moving the outhouses, though. It's been done too many times. They'd be expecting it." He turned his gaze to the sky where a crescent moon emerged from the clouds flitting by. "There she is, lass. Smiling down on us again. She will always have the last laugh on us mere mortals, I'm afraid."

TWENTY-THREE

The next day was Liam's favorite day of the week. On Sundays, not only could he sleep in until eight, but most of the morning was his to enjoy alone. Ginny and the children would be at church until half past ten, giving him time to prepare a hearty breakfast for the family to enjoy when they returned. Cooking was a pleasure that he only indulged in on this day.

Regarding church, he didn't need to make a special trip to enjoy the Creator's presence: it was everywhere to be enjoyed. The curve of Ginny's cheek, Rose's snapping blue eyes and Sean's patient resolve were gifts that he could cherish every day. The only bone he had to pick with the good Lord, and it was a bitter one, was the loss of his eldest child. But even he had to admit that the damned war had taken many fine lads.

As he busied himself frying bacon and left-over potatoes, Rose's tale of how old Mrs. Bennett had suffered embarrassment when William Pratt centered her out, rumbled in his head. It wasn't right to treat people the way the Pratts did. What was more galling was the fact that William Pratt always got away with it. People were wary of insulting the

Pratts because they needed to carry a running tab at the store until they got their paycheck.

He smiled thinking of the time he'd caught Wiley Will with his thumb on the weight scale when the young Foster woman was buying some meat. William's face bloomed like a ripe tomato when Liam had asked Sara Foster how she normally cooked William Pratt's fat thumb, since it was on the scale with the meat. He'd been affronted and then got really riled up when Sara laughed. Everyone knew it was true, that you had to watch Pratt like a hawk. Yet, he was probably glad handing everyone at church that very morning, making a show of flipping a five-dollar bill into the collection plate, like he was some kind of saint.

He'd speak to Ginny about sending Rose into the store. The next time she needed some groceries, Liam would buy them, with cash. They'd never had to run a tab at the store even though there were times when they did without, waiting for his paycheck from the town office.

When he heard Ginny's voice out front bidding good morning to a neighbor, Liam set the bacon aside to start the eggs. Rose was the first one through the door, the headscarf she'd worn to church already off and in her hand.

"Smells good, Daddy! I'm starving!" She grinned at him as she held the door for Sean to angle his crutch and come through the opening.

"Hi Da." Sean made his way to the table and set his crutch to the side as he took a seat. "The minister was really wound up today. He took the Sermon On The Mount to new heights of glory before he fell right over the cliff. You would have loved it."

Ginny cuffed the back of her son's head as she walked by, "Don't be disrespectful. There's enough of that from your father." She smiled as she planted a kiss on Liam's cheek. "Need some help?" She moved him aside and began to slice up a loaf of bread.

Liam's chest filled with love as he gazed at Ginny, slicing bread and popping them into the toaster. Her hands were delicate and swift as butterflies while her dark eyes twinkled as she worked. The years had been as kind to her as she was with everyone and everything. It was hard to believe that she'd ever agreed to marry him— a beautiful, educated lass falling for a poor farmer. So poor, that the Great Depression had finished that way of life.

Rose broke through his reverie when she asked, "Is it okay if I go over to Eve's after breakfast? She has a new dress pattern that she wants to work on. Her Mom's going to let us use the sewing machine."

Ginny looked over at Liam, trying to hide the smile on her face from her daughter. "You're sure it's Eve you're going to see and not her brother, Mark? I saw him with them in church today. He must be on some kind of furlough from the military."

Sean murmured as he poured a glass of milk. "I wonder how Robbie Smith will like *that?*"

Rose's cheeks were just like her namesake—a pretty pink—when she turned on her brother, "That's none of your concern, Sean. You'd better be careful or I'll have a chat with Mary Griffin. I'm sure she'd want to know that you're drawing pictures of her, when you're not writing poems about her glorious beauty."

Ginny turned and gave each of her children an icy stare. "Enough with that foolishness. You're fourteen, Rose and Sean's just turned sixteen, too young to be interested in romance. Pay more attention to your schoolwork. And yes, you may go to Eve's as long as your homework is done, Rose."

Liam sidled closer to Ginny and whispered in her ear. "You weren't much older than Rose when I sneaked a kiss at the county fair. It seems to me that you didn't mind it too much." Seeing her smile he put his arm around her waist and waltzed her over the floor, singing, "Ain't misbehaving, or fooling around, da da da da da—" |

Ginny burst into laughter and giving Liam a little push, she stepped away, "Go on with you, you crazy man!"

He tugged a lock of her ebony hair, "Crazy about you."

And it was absolutely the truth. It was as true now as the day he'd first saw her in her straw hat, watching as he'd shown his prize heifer.

Rose had been watching them with a grin lighting up her face, "Did you two go dancing much when you were young? I can't wait for my first dance!"

Liam began to dish out the breakfast he'd prepared. He pulled a face when he looked over at his daughter. "What do you mean, when we were young? We aren't fossils yet, young lady."

Ginny poured coffee, and the family sat down to their Sunday ritual. She looked over at Liam. "And what are your plans for the day, as if I didn't know? Cards with your buddies down at the garage? Just don't sample too much of Lester's beer and be home for dinner at five. I'm cooking your favorite, roast chicken."

Liam sipped his coffee, gazing over the rim at his wife of over twenty years. She knew him too well. Sunday cards with Lester, Alf, Ron and Hal were a staple in his life, like meat and potatoes. The only thing she didn't know was that sometimes they'd bet. So far, he'd been lucky. He just hoped his luck would hold out, and she'd never find out. She would tolerate the odd nip of beer or whiskey, but not gambling. But it was harmless, betting pennies for fun.

But there was another reason he wanted to visit his friends. Halloween was coming up and there was one family long overdue for a serious prank—the Pratts.

TWENTY-FOUR

ater that week Liam was on his way home from mopping the floors and emptying the garbage at the local school when he came upon Lizzie Bennett with her daughter, Lisa in tow. She had just come out of the Pratt's store and he could tell even from fifty feet away that she was fit to be tied, with two angry red spots flaring on her cheeks.

With her head down and stomping fast, she almost passed by him without a word, until he spoke. "Lizzie? Lizzie Bennett, you look like you've got a bee in your bonnet." He touched her arm gently, "What's wrong, lass?"

There were tears welling in her eyes when she looked at Liam, "I paid my bill at the store, Liam. I pay it every two weeks, as soon as I get my money."

Liam's eyes opened wider, "Well that's good! You should be proud that—"

"But it's not enough! It never is. He says I still owe him four dollars and sixty-two cents. That's four dollars that I don't have." She glanced at her daughter and then leaned closer, her voice barely above a whisper. "William Pratt told me that if I don't pay the balance in two weeks time then he's cutting my credit. I honestly don't know how the bill got so high. What am I going to do? We barely manage as it is."

Liam took the sack of groceries from her and then shepherded her along the walkway, going with her. "You don't have to worry about food, Lizzie. If you run low on something, just let me know. You've got friends and neighbors who won't stand by and see your youngsters go without." He looked over at her and his voice became lower, "You said you don't know how the charges at the store got so high."

She nodded and swiped a tear from her cheek. "That's right, I don't know. Granted, the kids are growing like weeds and we go through buckets of milk and bread, but still... I don't understand how the grocery bill got away from me. I'll never catch up, not on what I make cleaning houses."

Liam chose his words carefully before he spoke. He didn't want to make Lizzie feel worse than she already did. "It's not your fault, Lizzie. Times are hard and William Pratt doesn't make things any easier, not by a long shot. He's been known to put his thumb on the scale, charging people more than what's fair."

"Don't I know it!" She stopped short and her mouth fell open. "You think he does the same with the charge accounts?"

Liam's lips pulled to the side, and he shrugged. "Maybe. All I'm saying is that it might be wise to write down everything that you buy from the store. At the end of two weeks when you go there to pay up, you can compare your list with his." He laid his hand on her shoulder and looked her in the eye. "But you won't be going there on your own. I will go with you. Do you understand?"

"You will?" The worry lines that had creased her forehead relaxed when he nodded. She took the sack of groceries from his hand and breathed a sigh of relief. "Thanks, Liam. You're a good man. I wish that William Pratt was half as good. I wouldn't be in this pickle."

"Your husband Gerry was a good man, Lizzie. If he were alive, I'm sure none of this would be happening." He smiled at her. "Don't worry about this. In my experience, things have a way of working out."

Liam patted Lizzie's daughter's head and then slid his hand over the girl's ear. With a theatrical flourish he held a penny before the girl's eyes. "Now look at that, will you! I pulled a copper from your ear!"

He smiled when the girl took it with one hand while the fingers on her other hand touched her ear. "How'd you do that, Mr. Gallagher?" The kid's eyes were as big as dinner plates.

"Do what? I just gave you what I found in your ear." He winked at the girl and then stepped away from them, heading across the street to his own house.

"Thanks, Liam! Say hi to Ginny for me!"

Liam waved. "Will do! Take care, Lizzie." When his head was turned so that neither Lizzie or her daughter could see, his eyes narrowed. There was no doubt in his mind that Wiley Willie had tried to pull the wool over Lizzie's eyes. The muscle in his jaw twitched thinking of the poor widow trying to feed her two kids, cleaning other people's houses just to make ends meet.

William Pratt would never change. He'd been a sniveling sneak in grade school when they'd first met, and he was still a thieving weasel. Liam looked forward to going to the store with Lizzie in two weeks' time.

TWENTY-FIVE

When Liam arrived home after his encounter with Lizzie, he was surprised to see the parish pastor having tea with Ginny and Rose in the front room. He hung his jacket and hat on the hook and took a seat on the sofa next to his wife. "Good afternoon, Pastor Riley. What brings ye to my humble abode?"

The minister cleared his throat and cast a nervous glance at Ginny, before he spoke. "It's about your caretaker work in the church."

Ginny's chin rose high, and she reached to squeeze Liam's hand before she spoke. "It seems that there are some parishioners who don't like the fact that the church employs a man who doesn't attend the services, Liam. They don't feel it's right, even though I, and our children too, never miss a Sunday."

Pastor Riley pushed his glasses higher on his nose and edged forward till he was perched on the edge of the wooden chair. "I'm afraid, that's right. As you know, the church relies on contributions from the parishioners and well…" His voice trailed off.

Liam knew exactly which parishioners were complaining. It was the same ones who made such a show of being pious and 'Christian' when they knew everyone was looking. Keeping his voice light, Liam spoke. "It seems to me there's something in the Bible about Jesus tossing out the money changers from the temple. Yet in your church, these money folks sit right up in the front pew. Has the Good Book undergone an edit, Pastor?"

The middle-aged pastor's face was normally florid, but hearing Liam's criticism made his face become even redder. He stammered, "You know that's not true, Liam. Every person going to church is equal in the eyes of the Lord."

"Ah… there's the rub. So if a man chooses to worship the Lord in the bounty of nature or in the bosom of his family, he's not as equal. That's it. It doesn't matter if that same man abides by the ten commandments, and treats others as he wishes to be treated—fair and honest."

"That's not what I'm saying at all, Liam. No one disputes the fact that you're a hard worker and you're honest as the day is long, or that you aren't a good man. I've never had any complaints about your work keeping the grounds tidy and the church spotless."

Ginny clucked and squeezed Liam's hand again. "I should say not. Who exactly is lodging this complaint, Pastor? Surely, it wouldn't be the same people who basically run this town, flaunting their wealth in people's faces. The same ones everyone needs to watch closely when they're shopping lest they be cheated out of an extra dime?"

Liam smiled inwardly at Ginny's defense. It didn't mean she wasn't going to urge him to attend church later, when they were alone, but for now, in front of the Pastor, she wouldn't cotton to criticism of her husband.

The pastor slumped in his chair. "Now, Mrs. Gallagher, you know I can't say who complained. That was said in confidence." He sneaked a look at Liam, "It doesn't help that you spend the Sabbath imbibing in liquor and gambling at cards. You know I can't condone that and I've told you so in the past."

"I guess you also don't condone Jesus making wine out of water and being friends with harlots and thieves."

The pastor stood up even before Liam finished talking. "Look! Would it kill you to come to Sunday service even once a month? I don't enjoy having to threaten you with losing your job, Liam. I'm trying to help you, man."

Liam also stood, towering over the shorter man by a good four inches. "You're trying to placate the family who gives the biggest donation to your coffers. And how do I know they contribute the most money? Why, they make sure that everyone knows it. Even the dogs and cats in the village know that, I'm sure!"

Rose had been quiet for all of the conversation but now she spoke, "Pastor Riley, you spoke at church about gossiping and how the good lord hates that. It seems to me, that's what the Pratts are doing to my father. Surely, you wouldn't engage in gossiping with them behind my father's back."

"It's not gossip when it's the truth, Rose." The pastor walked across the room to the door and paused. "This isn't my decision, Liam. The Elders of the church meet at the end of the month and I'm sure this will come up. I just wanted to give you a head's up about this." He nodded to Ginny, murmuring his thanks for the tea. With that done, he went out the door.

Immediately, Rose jumped to her feet. "I'm never going back to that church if they give you the sack, Dad!"

"Me either!" Sean's voice was followed by his hesitant footsteps on the stairs, coming down to join them.

Ginny threw her hands in the air. "That'll be enough out of both of you! This is a discussion for adults, not children. Liam, let's go into the kitchen."

"I'm fourteen! I'm old enough to decide about church myself. If Dad doesn't need to go, neither do I."

"That goes for me as well." Sean joined his sister in protesting their mother's announcement.

Liam could tell by the stiff way that Ginny stormed out of the room that she was beyond angry. It didn't help his case that the children were using this to boycott their own church attendance. He signaled with his hands for the youngsters to keep quiet and then followed his wife to the other room.

Ginny banged the lid of the pot down and then plunked both onto the burner of the stove. Liam took a deep breath, seeing her slam the cutlery drawer after taking utensils out. She had to be really angry to act like that. But when she turned to him and blurted, "Those damned Pratts!" he felt his chest grow lighter. She was angry at them, not him, thank goodness. Ginny could be a spitfire when she got riled up.

He walked over to her and folded her into his arms. "If it will help, I'll go to church with you on Sunday. I need that job, Ginny."

She pushed away and looked into his eyes. "No, you won't! As far as that job goes, let them fire you! I'll be damned if those Pratts are going to dictate how you live your life." Her voice softened, "Not that I'd mind you going to church with us, but not like this. And if you lose your job, then we'll go to the other church, the Anglican one. At least the Pratts don't attend there, so that's a plus."

When Liam gazed at his wife, he thought his heart would burst with the overflowing love he felt. It didn't hurt that her cheeks were flushed like when she'd been a young girl and her eyes sparked with passion. He pulled her closer and stroked her satiny hair. "It won't come to that, love. Pratt is only one voice in the council of Elders. The rest are good lads. They know and like me. Besides which, Wiley Willie is due for a fall. I have a feeling that's coming sooner rather than later."

TWENTY-SIX

Saturday morning was always a busy time at the Pratt's general store. People who had been paid needed to settle accounts and lay in supplies for the next week. That was the reason that Liam had forestalled Lizzie O'Brien the day before, when normally she'd pay her bill and stock up at the store.

Standing across the street, he smoked his pipe, watching friends and neighbors filing in. In his pocket was the list of items that Lizzie had written of the groceries she'd bought on credit for the previous two weeks. She'd also included the sum of cash that would take care of it, as well as a dollar to put on her outstanding balance.

Liam tipped his hat to the post mistress, Beverly Potter, as she walked by him, on her way to get her groceries. He smiled watching her and emptied the bowl of his pipe onto the ground. He'd been waiting specifically for Mrs. Potter who was the hub of information, handling the mail and gossiping with practically anyone who had the time to listen. Inside the store, the stage was set for Liam to make an entrance.

The bell above the door jingled when Liam walked in. He

glanced over at Wiley Willie Pratt who stood behind the counter, ringing through Ida Walker with her purchases. When William saw Liam, the slimy smile on his face fell like a stone. That was good. This wasn't a social call and the feeling between the two men was mutual, even if Liam could camouflage his disdain with a pleasant greeting. "Morning Willie, Mrs. Walker. It's a fine autumn day."

A quick scan of the store showed about a dozen people chatting or picking up items they needed and putting them into cloth satchels or wicker baskets. When Mrs. Walker was through at the counter, Liam stepped right up to take her place.

William Pratt's gaze was frigid, taking in the fact that Liam stood there empty-handed. "Did you forget what your wife sent you in for, Liam? If you don't mind, it's busy and other people need my help. You should bring a list next time." William Pratt was about to step away, but Liam's response stopped him cold.

"I'm here on Lizzie Bennett's behalf. Lizzie was feeling poorly and asked me to bring her money in to settle her bill." Liam paused and glanced around at the people shopping. Raising his voice a little, he continued, "Poor Lizzie was worried that you were going to make good on your threat to cut off her credit."

William's eyes opened wider and his gaze darted to his customers, while Liam's lips twitched, trying to hide his smirk.

But William recovered quickly from his embarrassment. "I assure you that would never happen, not that it's any of your business, Liam. You'd do well to pay more attention to your own family. I see Rose with her friend Eve hanging out at the garage where the young men gather to smoke."

"If you sell spectacles, you might want to try a pair for yourself, Willie. The only teens hanging out there are your own two. But that isn't why I've come in here today. As I said, Lizzie Bennett asked me to settle her account. How much does she owe, Willie?"

William sighed and reached under the counter for his black

ledger. He flipped a few pages and then his finger slid down the one he'd paused at. "Twelve dollars and fourteen cents, not counting the four, sixty-four she already owed."

Liam's head pulled back and his forehead knotted. "Is that so? Are you sure about that amount?" It was so hard to play this out without grinning. He glanced around, delighted to see that people had quieted even though they picked up items, scanning the labels, pretending to be busy with their own shopping.

William let out an exasperated sigh. "Of course, I'm sure. This is my livelihood, working with numbers. Unlike you, my work involves mental skills, not pushing a broom or picking up other people's garbage."

Liam let out a short laugh. "That's right. You're a real genius, aren't you? It's a shame the university didn't think so. After all your bragging about studying to become a doctor and yet, here you are, a shopkeeper."

William's blustered, trying to pass off Liam and turn to other customers. Liam pulled Lizzie's list of purchases from his pocket and plopped it down on the counter.

Tapping it with his forefinger, he smiled at William. His voice again was louder than he normally spoke. "Lizzie made this list of things she'd got from your store over the past two weeks. According to her reckoning, she owes ten dollars and eighty-two cents. That's a difference of one dollar and thirty-two cents or as a percentage, it's a little over ten percent."

You could hear a pin drop in the store when Liam finished talking. William's eyes were narrow slits when he snatched the list up, scowling at it. "Obviously, there are items that Mrs. Bennett didn't record here."

"Or items that you recorded that never made it to Lizzie's house. It's a small wonder that you told her she has an outstanding balance. Lizzie couldn't understand how that came to be, but I think I know the answer to that riddle."

Liam turned slightly to speak to the people who now openly stared at the exchange. "It costs money to go gallivanting across the lake in a new motorboat. I'm getting a good idea how the Pratts are able to afford that boat."

"How dare you imply that my accounting is dishonest? I don't have to listen to this. Tell Lizzie Bennett to come in herself and settle her bill, not send some old drunken janitor in to insult me." William slammed the accounting book shut and then tossed the list back at Liam. "Get out of my store."

Liam's eyes became wide, and he blinked a few times, staring at William. "Me thinks thou doth protest too much! That's from Shakespeare, Willie, in case you were wondering." He snorted, "Lizzie will pay the amount that's owed according to her own honest notes. You will take that money right now and these good folks will bear witness that her bill is paid."

Just at that moment, the door opened, and Rose with her friend Eve walked into the store. Rose started to say something, but a look at her father and the other people staring at William Pratt kept her silent.

"Well? Are you going to take this money to settle the bill or should I make it my business to let the entire town know they should check their accounts? Ten percent above the bill is a lot of money to folks in this town." Liam stepped closer to the counter and pounded his fist down. "What's it going to be, Wiley Willie?"

A snicker broke out behind Liam and was quickly joined by another and another. The postmistress chimed in, "If this is true that we're all being over-charged then maybe the Pratts should take every one of us for a ride in that fancy boat of theirs."

The door at the side of the store leading up to the Pratt's living quarters opened and Edith Pratt walked in. She was just in time to hear the last of Beverly Potter's comment about the boat. "What's going on? Why would we take anyone out in our boat? If you want a boat ride, work hard and then you can buy one for yourself."

It was the spark that lit up the crowd of people waiting to purchase their groceries. Liam practically crowed with joy when Beverly Potter answered the Pratt woman.

"We DO work hard, but it seems you and your family

benefit from our labor more than we do." The large woman turned to the other people, who were also murmuring their agreement. "You'd do well to copy Lizzie Bennett's idea to keep your own accounting of what you buy here. I can understand the odd discrepancy, but ten percent suggests more than an error in arithmetic."

Liam watched William's face flare as red as a cranberry, an over-ripe one that could explode at any moment. It was Pratt's wife who addressed the crowd. "I welcome anyone to look at William's accounting. You will find that all is in order. Please, can't we get along like the Good Book advises? We're neighbors for goodness sakes!"

Liam thrust his hand into his pocket and withdrew Lizzie's money. He made a big show of counting out every coin and dollar note, slapping them down on the wooden counter. All the while, he could hear the hiss of William's breath, breathing through his nose while his jaw muscle clenched.

Rose stepped over to her father, "Daddy? Mom needs some vanilla extract. Will you wait while I grab a bottle?"

"Of course, dear. I'll be right here waiting." Liam spoke to his daughter, but his gaze never left Pratt's face. He lowered his voice, leaning over the counter, "If I were you, I'd tear up that over-drawn entry of the four dollars and change that you said Lizzie owes. There was a time that crooked dealings would end up with a man wearing tar and feathers. Count yourself lucky that those times are gone."

William snatched the money from the counter and tossed it into his till. "You're a drunken trouble maker, Gallagher. If you cause any more problems in my store, I'll call the constable and have you forcibly removed."

Rose and Eve appeared with the spice, and Liam paid for it from money in his other pocket. He sneered at Wiley Willie, "You mean your cousin, don't you? It's easy for you to throw your weight around having a first cousin in the police force isn't it?" Liam snorted. "And speaking of weight, Ed has a hard time fitting into that car of his, let alone toss me out. He's as crooked as you are, Willie."

"You can't talk to my husband like that!"

Ignoring Edith Pratt, Liam turned to face his neighbors and friends, removing his cap with a flourish and taking a low bow. "So ends this farcical play. Enjoy what is left of the weekend and watch your pennies when you shop here."

When he stepped outside, Rose came right beside him, looping her arm through his. "You sure showed that mean old Pratt, Daddy."

Eve looked up at him. "You stirred up a hornet's nest in there, Mr. Gallagher!"

He smiled down at the girls. "And that I did! Now run the vanilla home while I stop to see Lizzie Bennett. She was worried about her bill at the store, but I think we fixed it for her. I'll be home as soon as I cut the grass at the church and get it ready for Sunday." Somehow, he had the feeling that after the scene in the store, few people would be swayed by William Pratt wanting to give him the sack from that job.

He thought of the red rage that had twisted Wiley Willie's face and let out a low chuckle.

TWENTY-SEVEN

A few hours later, with the church ready for the Sunday services the next day, Liam trudged home. As tempting as it was to pop by Hank's house for a bottle of beer and a chat, he was just too weary. When he opened the door and saw Ginny at the kitchen table, snapping green beans, preparing them for dinner, he knew in an instant she was angry. He could read her face better than his own.

Seeing a wisp of steam drifting from the spout of the teapot, he poured a cup and took a seat at the table. "You heard about the dust up in the store, I take it."

She paused holding a bean with her two hands. Her eyes sparked, "Yes. Rose told me some of what went on. You paid Lizzie Bennett's bill and there was some discrepancy? Rose said the store was packed full of people."

He took a sip and then set the cup down gently. "Technically, it was Lizzie's money. She had a list of her purchases for the past two weeks which didn't match Wiley Willie's. It was out by almost two dollars, Ginny. That's a lot for someone like Lizzie, as you know."

Ginny's shoulders slumped, and she reached for his hand.

"Yes. I know. But you've made things worse between us and the Pratt's, Liam. If there were another store closer, I'd go there in a heartbeat, but we're stuck." She pulled her hand back and went back to her task. "Please promise me you'll stay away from the Pratts. Rose or I will do the shopping from now on. I don't like the Pratts either, but we have to try to live with them. It's not that big a village, Liam."

Liam hated arguing with Ginny. He's just as soon cut off his right hand than be on the outs with her, but he couldn't go along with what she wanted. "I won't cower away from them, Ginny. They are the ones in the wrong here, taking advantage of a poor widow and God knows how many other folks who pay on credit. Someone needs to stand up to them."

Ginny leaned closer, lowering her voice, "I'm not defending them. They are mean-spirited, horrid people. Just don't add fuel to the fire. That's all I'm asking."

Liam smiled. "You should have seen Willie's face, Ginny. I thought he'd blow a gasket, sputtering and yelling at me. But the best was when people started snickering about what was going on. He detests it when people laugh at him."

She shook her head even though a smile played on her lips. "That would please you, to see him shamed like that. He's a stuffed shirt who thinks he's better than the rest of us." Her smile dropped, and she wagged a finger at him, "But that's the end of it. No riling him up any more or playing any of your pranks on him at Halloween. Are we clear?"

Liam cupped the teacup in both hands, gazing at her. "Why... I thought I'd take you for a ride in their new boat at Halloween. At least before I set it adrift, that is. It might end up at Rideau Ferry for all I know. That'd be a good one on them."

"No. I know you like Halloween but leave them alone. Go play cards and have a drink with your friends. You know I'm serious when I'm telling you to do that! I don't trust William Pratt or his shrewish wife. Their kids are not much better." She set her hands on the table, pleading with him with her eyes. "Please, for my sake and the children's, let this go, Liam. I'm watching and if you do anything to make matters worse, I will be angry."

Liam didn't answer her. She was already angry. But he'd seen Ginny get a bee in her bonnet a few times before and she always got over it. He'd think about what she'd asked, but that was as far as he was willing to go. No promises. It would depend on how things went over the next while. His Halloween pranks had been a tradition of his for years and years, and if there was one person who deserved a 'trick' it was Wiley Willie. But it would be the first time that he hadn't pulled a hilarious prank on Halloween. That would be hard to resist.

TWENTY-EIGHT

It was the last Tuesday of the month, a night that normally wouldn't be remarkable to Liam. But much as he'd tried to downplay his concern about losing the caretaker job at the church, it had played in the back of his mind. As he stood outside in his yard, he wondered how the Elder's meeting tonight would be decided.

He was pretty sure he could count on Dan Jones, Harold Smith (Alf's father) and Ernie Adams for their support, but Willie Pratt had his allies as well. Of course, his cousin the constable would side with Willie. Alderman Wyatt, a newcomer to the village, was chummy with the Pratts. That left the deciding vote to old man Humphrey. Half the time the septuagenarian couldn't tell you what day of the week it was, let alone decide on an issue like this.

The back door banged shut, and he looked over to see Rose darting across the grass towards him. Her blonde hair caught a breath of wind and lifted from the shoulders of her green wool coat. Even in the low light of the evening her eyes sparked and there was a smile itching on her smooth face.

"Finished helping your Ma with the clean-up, Darlin'?" It

was the same thing he asked every evening that it was fine enough to go outside. He waited for her to spill whatever devilment had put an extra spring in her step.

"The dishes are all done and put away, Daddy." She stood next to him, leaning over the fence watching the street and the waterfront behind it. Finally she looked up at him and grinned. "Robbie Smith got into a fistfight with James Pratt after school today. You should have seen it; he gave him a bloody nose." She looked away and her voice became softer, "Robbie was sticking up for me."

Liam's eyebrows arched high before he made a show of lighting his pipe. The shy pride in Rose's voice told him more about her genuine feelings for what the Smith lad had done for her than anything else. She was growing up, becoming more of a woman every day. "What did James Pratt do that Robbie had to clean his clock for him?"

Rose looked up at him. "It wasn't what he did, but what he said. He's been even more of a drip than usual since you had that set-to with his father. He was making fun of my clothes, asking me what trash bin I got my dress from. He said it even smelled like garbage, that maybe you found it in the dump for me."

Liam's breath froze in his chest as he listened to his daughter. The feud between William Pratt and him was one thing, but having it spill over so that his youngsters were hurt and embarrassed was quite another. If James Pratt were there, he'd box his ears so bad he wouldn't hear anything for a week! But he puffed his pipe, keeping his voice calm. "I'm glad that Robbie taught him a lesson, Rose. That's a cruel thing to say to a young lady. Your mother made you that dress and it's a dandy. Pay no attention to James Pratt."

She snorted. "I don't. No one does, really, except for Jack Ainslie and his cousin Mike. They just hang around him for the candy he always has in his lunch. But that's not the problem, Daddy."

Liam put his hand on Rose's head, stroking her hair. "What is then? It sounds to me that the problem was solved and right handily by Robbie Smith."

She sighed. "It's Eve. She's had a crush on Robbie since grade one. I tried to pass Robbie's defending me as just being nice but she said it was that he likes me. She ran home in tears and she wouldn't come to the door when I stopped at her house."

Oh, the trials of young love. Liam put his thumb under Rose's chin and turned her face up to look her in the eyes. "Eve Thatcher is a lovely girl. You've been friends since the time you both could walk. And you grew closer still when we moved to the village. But Rose... you can't control how Robbie feels. It would be easier if he felt the same way about Eve as she does about him, but apparently... and according to your brother, he's smitten with you."

Rose pulled away and then kicked at the fence board. "I know. I didn't ask him to like me! I like Eve a whole lot better than I like Robbie Smith! She won't even speak to me, Daddy."

"Hold on, girl. There's no call to beat up the fence. You might have to tell Robbie that you don't care for him in the way he cares about you. That may cool his ardor. As for Eve, she may never get over this. All you can do is keep trying to be her friend." He tugged her hair, "It wouldn't hurt to put a bug in Robbie's ear that Eve likes him. Sometimes boys need a nudge from the fairer sex to set them on the right track."

He thought of Ginny asking him to ease off teasing Willie Pratt and making things worse. She'd been trying to set him on the right track, but instead of a nudge, she'd given him a flat out kick. He still hadn't decided what he was going to do about that. It depended on how things went with that Elders meeting.

Rose looked up at him and flashed a small smile. "I'll try to make it up to Eve." She stepped away from the fence. "I'd better go finish my reading assignment."

"I thought you said it was done."

"Nope. I said I helped with the cleaning up." She squeezed his hand. "Thanks, Daddy."

Liam sighed. If only life was that easy to fix with a few

words. As far as Robbie was concerned, the lad was all right in his books. At least he'd stuck up for Rose against James Pratt.

Hearing footsteps coming down the street, Liam peered in the low light to see who it might be. He smiled seeing that it was Harold Smith ambling towards him. Liam pulled his pocket watch from his trousers and noted the time. The Elders meeting had ended early. Was that a good sign?

Harold waved and trotted over to where Liam stood. His face was hard to read before he flashed a smile. "Pratt was voted down, Liam. Old Mr. Humphrey couldn't attend which was probably a good thing for you. It took the pastor's voice weighing in to decide that your work merited keeping you on. He sermonized at length about 'judge not, lest ye be judged'. Not that his words carried any weight with William Pratt."

Liam let out a sigh of relief as his grip on the fence loosened. The weight of losing that job had been lifted from his shoulders—a weight that he hadn't realized wore on him so much. He reached for Harold's hand and shook it. "Thanks, Harold. I know you were on my side."

Harold laughed, "Just remember this the next time we play cards. Don't cheat and take all my pennies!"

Liam clapped him on the shoulder, "You need a better poker face is all, Harold! I'll see you Saturday."

He stood there for a long while after Harold left, whistling a cheery tune. Wiley Willie would be fit to be tied after losing that vote. It would be all over town, compounding the embarrassment that Liam had caused him a couple weeks ago that Saturday at the store.

The hurtful teasing that Rose had suffered at James Pratt's hands was a cloud dampening his joy at keeping the job. And to make matters worse for his daughter, her best friend was now on the outs with her. He hated that his kids were paying the price of his battles with the Pratts.

He let out a long sigh, staring at the sky and the crescent moon. This feud had to stop.

Ginny had asked him to lay off and then Rose had been hurt. He would never be friends with old Pratt but at least there could be a truce. It would gall him to do it, but he had his family to think of. He'd meet with Wiley Willie and try to make amends—not become friends, of course—but they could at least be civil to one another. He'd tell Ginny after the deed was done.

TWENTY-NINE

Ginny and Sean were dipping apples into a caramel sauce when Liam came home from work on Friday. A bowl of popcorn balls wrapped in waxed paper sat on the sideboard, waiting to be doled out to the children trick or treating later. He was a bit later than usual as he'd had to stack the tables and chairs off to the side for the Halloween dance at the community hall that had Rose all abuzz.

"Merry Christmas, Sean! I see you're helping your mother stuff the Christmas stockings." He ruffled his son's hair as he walked by and then gave Ginny a kiss on her cheek.

"Da! You know it's Halloween! I can tell by the mask you're wearing!" Sean ducked when Liam went to cuff him on the side of his head.

"Smart Alec! Don't laugh, you get your homely face from me, boy!" He dipped his finger in the sauce and then sampled it. "You're shelling out with your Ma?"

Ginny started to say something about Liam helping out with that too, when Rose and Eve burst into the room, giggling like well... schoolgirls.

Rose pirouetted twirling the edges of her long skirt in a circle around her calves. She had fashioned a tiara using foil and cardboard that sat squarely on her blonde hair. She wore her mother's pearls over the blue satin dress and there were fobs fastened to her earlobes. "How do I look? Like a Princess?"

Liam bowed low, extending his arm in a sweep. "Your Royal Silliness!" When he rose, he clutched his arms over his chest, edging away from Eve who was dressed in a black dress with a pointed witch's hat perched on her head. "Don't turn me into a toad! I promise, I'll give you candy apples, popcorn and caramels if you leave me be!"

Eve flushed a bright pink and looked at the floor. "You're silly, Mr. Gallagher." She looked up at him, "Maybe a newt? I think you'd make a good newt."

Liam laughed. It was good to see that the two girls had made up after their kerfuffle with the Smith boy. Rose hadn't said if she'd talked to Robbie but he hoped she had. They didn't need any more friction between them. "So you two are off to the dance soon? Aren't you going to miss trick or treating and getting a sack of candy?"

Rose swept across the floor, still hamming it up. "It is decreed that there shall be copious amounts of candy at the dance. The teachers and some parents chaperoning will bring some."

Liam huffed. "Why didn't they ask me to chaperone? I could use some candy."

"Ya Dad. You need something to sweeten you up." Again, Sean was quick in dodging Liam's finger flick.

"Why don't you give us a lift to the school?" Rose lifted her foot showing her mother's high heel shoe and grimaced. "These things will be the death of me. How can women wear them?"

Ginny's eyes opened wider, seeing her good shoes on Rose's feet. "Don't break the heel or your ankle, young lady. Be careful. Maybe your father could give you a lift in the car." She turned to Liam, "Then come right back, Mister. No wandering around pulling any pranks."

"Me? Why, I'm as innocent as the driven snow, Ginny." Liam smiled thinking how this would fit in with his plan. What better time to make amends than on Halloween? Not even

Wiley Willie could spoil his pleasant mood on this night. The store would be closed and it would give them privacy for their conversation.

Dinner was catch as catch can that night. Liam helped himself to a ham sandwich; he was forced to it gobble down when Rose and Eve showed signs of impatience.

He wiped his face and then rose from the table. "C'mon ladies. The dance won't be able to commence without the belles of the ball arriving." As he hustled the girls out the front door, he noticed Sean watching quietly. It was sad to see his son missing out on the dance but quite understandable he'd want to forgo it, given his bum leg. He winked at his son, "Save me one of those candy apples, Sean. I'll see you later."

When he pulled up outside the school in his automobile, there were a few students milling around outside the open door. Robbie Smith broke with the boys he stood with to head over to the car and open the door for Rose and Eve. Liam smiled at the three of them and called out, "Have fun tripping the light fantastic". The looks they shot him before they turned to join their friends showed they had no idea what he'd just said. He chuckled. Just because he had never finished high school didn't mean he had stopped reading and learning.

He took a deep breath and steered the car back onto the street, rounding the block to head for the Pratt's store. He'd put this off for the last couple of days and it was time to get this over with. As he drove down the street, he watched for youngsters out trick or treating, caught up in the fun and not paying attention. It didn't help that darkness had descended, making it more difficult to see the little rascals.

Parking the car in front of the store, he hesitated for just a few moments before getting out. The side door which led to the Pratt's residence was lit by the overhead light, but other than that all was dark in the store itself. When he walked up the walkway to their house, he heard a banging and muffled voices coming from around the house in their backyard. It sounded like Willie and another male voice.

He rounded the corner of the house and saw two dark

shapes, one on the dock and the other one, much shorter, was in the motorboat tied there. They continued talking, unaware that he was walking across the grass towards them.

"This ought to discourage any pranksters fooling around with the boat, Dad."

Liam's eyebrows rose. If not for Ginny and his children, there would be nothing he'd enjoy more than setting that boat adrift and seeing the Pratt's anger at losing it. But that wouldn't happen.

He stepped onto the dock and called to them. "William? It's Liam Gallagher. I want to talk to ye."

"What are you doing on my property? You're here to try some trick, but I'm two steps ahead of you, you old fool. Get off my dock or I'll have the law on you." William took a step closer to his boat and son.

"Calm down, Willie. I'm not here to pull any pranks on you or your boat. As I said, I want to have a few words with you." Liam walked slowly across the wooden structure watching Willie and his own footing. The boards were slippery with the moist air and damp. For just a few moments he regretted not having this conversation in the daylight. He pulled his box of matches from his pocket and lit one, lighting his way slightly.

"There's nothing a washed up janitor like you could say that I'd even be remotely interested in hearing. Go home and leave us god-fearing people in peace, you reprobate." Willie's voice wavered just a little, and he took a step back as Liam approached.

Liam could tell that Willie was uncomfortable, if not downright jittery seeing him on his dock at nightfall. He had to swallow the retort that threatened to leap from his tongue, especially to Willie's comment about them being 'god fearing people'. Self-righteous hypocrites was more accurate.

His son James chimed in, "You heard my dad, you smelly, Garbage-Gallagher. Get out of here."

Liam's jaw tightened, and he counted to ten, trying to keep his tongue in check. "I'm here to call a truce in our relationship, William. There's no need of name-calling. We're adults and this is between us." He stopped when he was about two feet away from William. He could just barely make out the man's narrow slits for eyes and his thin lips drawn tight.

"There's no relationship that I want to have between us, not unless it's my foot landing on the seat of your britches when I kick you off this dock. You're lucky I even allow your family in my store to shop." Again, Willie's voice held a little waiver, and he shuffled his feet, edging back a bit.

"I'm trying to be reasonable, Willie. All I'm asking is that you meet me half-way. We will never be friends but we don't have to be mortal enemies either. I will treat you as fairly as you are willing to treat me. Deal?" Liam extended his hand, even though every fiber of his being wanted to use that hand to give Willie a jab in his gob. He forced himself to think of Ginny and his children. This was necessary for their peace of mind.

The offer of his hand in a show of peace went unanswered. The next thing he knew there was a whoosh of air before a blasting pain exploded in his head. He stumbled forward, going down on his knees. He grabbed for Willie's hand but the other man had jumped back. For a moment as he hunched over trying to push up despite the pain, he saw stars fill his vision.

"That'll teach him Dad! You warned him, but he wouldn't listen. I got him good with the paddle."

The youngster's voice felt like it was coming from a long dark tunnel. Liam's hand rose to feel the back of his head. There was a pounding goose-egg there and his fingers were sticky when he pulled them away. Again, he struggled, trying to keep his balance while pushing himself higher.

"Take that, Gallagher!"

Willie's voice accompanied another pummeling arc of pain. Liam was knocked over when William kicked him. The last thing he saw before everything went black was William winding up to kick him again.

His last thought was Ginny's face, fading as his eyes closed.

Present Day...

THIRTY

Sharon leaned closer to Eve Smith. "What do you mean, 'you saw a ghost'? That was James Pratt leaving my house. Did you know the Pratts at one time?" Sharon examined the old woman's face, trying to read the lines to get an idea of the woman's age. She could be in her nineties, but if that was the case, she was sharp for someone that old.

Eve turned and despite the watery blue of her eyes, she fixed Sharon in a stare. "Everyone knew the Pratts. But it was the Gallaghers who I knew better. Rose and I were best friends growing up." She turned to stare at Sharon's house across the street. "I've seen families come and go, seen the addition put on to the side of that house. That house was my second home when I was a lass."

Peter spoke, "So you knew Liam and the Pratts who ran the store? You were here when Liam drowned that Halloween?" He glanced at Sharon before turning back to the old woman.

She was silent for a few moments and a slight smile played on her thin lips. "I will never forget that Halloween. It was not only my first dance, it was the night I received my first kiss." She let out a chuckle as she looked down at her lap. "I married that sweet boy. But Rob's been dead these past twenty years."

As sweet as this memory was for the old lady, Sharon's curiosity got the better of her. "But what about Liam? And Rose and Ginny and Sean?" She shook her head as she looked over at Lillian, "All this time we've been searching, picking your aunt's brain and the answers were here across the street from me."

"Unbelievable, but Aunt Mary is a lot younger..." She glanced at Eve Smith before she continued. "She tends to stick with her own set of friends. I guess her memory isn't as good as she thinks." Lillian shrugged and then turned to look at Eve Smith again.

Eve finished taking a sip of water and then handed the glass to her caretaker. "Where was I? Yes... Rose and me."

"Actually, we'd like to know about Liam's death. I found a note that I think was written by Rose. She stated that her father's death wasn't an accident." Sharon was eager to hear the story, but given Eve's age, she needed to be gentle in her probing.

Eve huffed, "No one in the village thought it was an accident. But it was William Pratt's cousin, the policeman, who headed up the investigation... if you'd even call it an investigation. He said that Liam must have been drinking when he trespassed on William's property. Of course, Liam had a reputation as a drinker as well as pulling pranks. So the story they pushed was that he'd been planning on doing something to the Pratt's boat."

"Did you see Liam at all that day? Could he have been drinking?" Peter asked.

Eve's eyes narrowed when she looked at him. "Liam drove Rose and me to the dance. He'd just got home from work and barely had time for a bite to eat before we nagged him into taking us. No. He was sober."

"Yet he was found drowned the next day. How do you think that happened?" Sharon was silent for a few moments, reliving the scene she'd experienced the day before when it felt like she'd been inside Liam's body as he was dying. "It was near the Pratt's dock, right?"

Eve nodded. "Just down from it. But why he'd be anywhere near the Pratt's is a mystery to me. When we got home that night from the dance, Liam wasn't there. I remember, Ginny Gallagher being fit to be tied. She assumed he was out with his friends pulling Halloween pranks."

Lillian spoke next, "My uncle told me that the village shunned the Pratts and their store after Liam drowned. Even though the village came out to support the Gallaghers, it still must have been difficult for them. Whatever happened to Rose and Sean?"

"Rose was never the same girl after her father died. She became bitter and the first chance she got, she left Westport. I heard she lived in Kingston for a while and then moved to Toronto. We lost touch with each other. Even Sean had a hard time finding her when it came time to settle the estate, when Ginny died. He didn't last much longer than his mother."

Eve's caretaker put her hand on the old woman's shoulder. "I think you need to rest now, Eve. This has taken a lot out of you."

The old woman seemed to shrink into herself when she nodded. "I am tired." She looked over at Sharon, "Seeing that young man, that Pratt today... it broke something inside me. I haven't thought of this in years. I'm sorry, but I must lie down for a bit."

Sharon stood up and patted Eve's shoulder. "No apology necessary. I'm glad that we had a chance to talk. Maybe we will again, when you're feeling up to it."

When Sharon, Peter and Lillian entered the house they went into the kitchen to have tea and talk. Sharon let Peter do the honors of making the tea while she sank down onto the chair. "What a sad way that the Gallaghers ended up. Liam's death ruined their lives."

Lillian sighed. "Yes. I'll have to ask Aunt Mary about Eve Smith."

Peter took a seat at the table, "But that was her married name. Your aunt might remember her by her maiden name."

His eyebrows arched, "... which we don't know as she didn't say."

Sharon sat quietly ruminating about James Pratt showing up at their door like that. Ignoring both of Lillian's and Peter's comments, she spoke, "She said it was like she'd seen a ghost when James stormed off. The family resemblance must be uncanny for her to react like that."

Peter looked over at her. "Maybe not just in appearances. James' reactions to your conversation and then today was over the top. I mean... coming up here to threaten us if we went near his wife again was a bit extreme."

"Extreme for us but maybe normal for him? His wife said he didn't take a joke very well. It sounds like he has a tendency to fly off the handle."

Peter added to Lillian's comment, "There's no way he will make a go of any kind of business in the village. Dealing with the public would be a serious challenge for someone like him."

Lillian looked at her watch before sighing. "I'm not sure I have time to help with this smudging thing, now. I need to help Aunt Mary. If you can wait—"

"No." Sharon looked over at Peter, "I don't want to do this. I might change my mind in a few days time if Liam pulls anything else, but for now, I just want to leave this alone. After hearing Eve Smith, it doesn't feel right."

Peter leaned closer to her, taking her hand, "What about Hannah coming home for the weekend? I thought you wanted all this over and done for that?"

Sharon felt as old as Eve Smith when she answered, "We'll talk to Hannah. Once she knows everything that's happened and what Eve told us, she'll understand. She's strong and even if Liam pulls a trick, she'll be okay. He never hurts us, just startles us every chance he gets."

When Lillian rose, Sharon walked her to the door. She peered across the street at Eve Smith's home, but the verandah was empty. "Thanks, Lillian. This has been quite a day, beating a path to the Reservation and then hearing what Eve Smith had to say. Maybe I will have to get used to Liam haunting this house."

Lillian shook her head. "I can understand how you feel. After all that Liam went through, it seems cruel to force him out of the house where he lived with his family. But I'll be honest... I don't like the fact that the Pratt descendant is back."

Sharon felt her chest tighten when she glanced down the street at the Pratt's house, "I don't either."

THIRTY-ONE

Sharon felt like her mind was going in ten different directions when she went back into the kitchen to join Peter. He was in the middle of a phone call. Her head jerked back, seeing Peter's smile as he held his cell phone to his ear. Seeing Sharon's puzzled look he mouthed the word 'Hannah' before he spoke, "Sure, That's great. See you soon." When he clicked the phone, ending the call he looked over at Sharon, "Hannah's on her way out. She got Friday off, so she wanted to get a jump on the weekend. She wangled a ride out with one of her friends."

"Oh." It was one more thing to deal with in a day that had held all kinds of surprises.

"What? You don't look so happy about her coming early. It is her birthday weekend, y'know. I think it will be a pleasant distraction from all that's been happening around here." Peter shook his head and then rose to take his mug to the dishwasher.

"I didn't mean it like that, Peter! Of course I'm happy she'd going to be with us early. It's just unexpected, that's all. I have to make her cake and I haven't even wrapped her birthday present with all that's been happening here." Sharon went over and put her arms around Peter's waist, snuggling into his back. "It was a crazy day."

He turned around and pulled her close, murmuring in her ear. "It's been a crazy week is more like it. Hannah will be surprised when we tell her about Eve Smith—especially after being snubbed by the old woman when she waved to her. I'd like to invite Eve over for coffee sometime."

Sharon looked around the room, "How about that, Liam? Your daughter's best friend has been living across the street from this house all these years."

Peter snorted, "Feel free to visit her anytime, Liam. How about this weekend while Hannah's home? It would be nice to have a visit with our daughter without you pulling any tricks. Think you can do that?"

"We'd better start getting dinner ready. Did Hannah say whether she'd eaten yet? I'll defrost some pork chops and bake them with stuffing." Sharon opened the freezer door of the fridge and rooted around looking for them.

"You better make it snappy because she said she was almost here when she called. She wondered if we needed anything." Peter cocked his ear and grinned. "She wasn't kidding. I think I just heard a car door bang shut."

Sharon set the meat in the sink and then followed Peter when he went to the front door. Sure enough, a compact silver car had pulled up to the sidewalk. Hannah finished saying goodbye to whoever was driving and emerged from the side door.

At the bang from down the street, followed by shouting, Sharon stepped by Peter to see. Her mouth fell open, seeing Sandy Pratt sprint to her SUV, yelling over her shoulder. James was only a few steps behind his wife, bellowing at her.

"What the heck?" Peter gaped as well at the commotion in the Pratt's driveway. Even Hannah dawdled, coming up the walkway and stairs. Her puzzled gaze flitted between the Pratts and her parents.

James Pratt had followed Sandy to the vehicle. He grabbed

her by the arm, but she yanked away and jumped in. He stood at the driver's side, banging on the roof. The engine roared to life and the vehicle backed out. Tires screeched on the pavement as she floored the gas, driving the vehicle past Sharon's house, barely missing Hannah's friend when he went to pull out onto the street.

Hannah's eyes were round when she turned to her parents. "Was that Sandy Pratt? She sure left in a hurry! Looks like they had one heck of a fight!"

Sharon blinked a few times, looking in the direction where Sandy had headed. The SUV rounded a bend in the street and disappeared from sight.

Peter took Hannah's backpack from her and muttered, "You don't know the half of it, Hannah. James Pratt... well, let's just say, he's not a nice guy."

"What happened? There's more to this. Spill it." Hannah grabbed her mother's arm, "I'm glad I came home early. What's been going on around here?"

Sharon took a deep breath and led her daughter into the house. "Well, the house is still haunted with Liam Gallagher's ghost for one thing. And James Pratt is angry with Lillian and me."

"Don't forget me! I'm pretty sure he's not my biggest fan. Remember, it was me who got an earful from him this afternoon." Peter added as he followed behind them.

Hannah let out a laugh. "Home sweet home. I can't wait to hear all about it."

THIRTY-TWO

James Pratt's blood pounded in his ears as he glared at the SUV peeling rubber up the street from his house. Seeing the Phelps' crew gawking from their verandah as Sandy made such a fool of herself and *him* only added fuel to the fire burning in his gut. This was that meddling bitch's fault—that stupid Sharon! He should have punched her weasel husband Peter in the mouth when he went to see them earlier. And now their daughter was home to add her two cents to the ruckus.

Screw them! And screw Sandy, too. He didn't need her sniveling around, siding with the neighbors against him. She was his *wife* for Christ's sake! The least she could do was show some loyalty. He stormed back into the house and his feet pounded on the stairs as he went up to their residence.

He saw the broken plate and the spaghetti strewn over the wooden floor. If not for the lump of noodles in a mound, the stream of red sauce spattered even up the newly painted wall looked like the scene of a slasher movie. He snorted. Maybe some of it was her blood. He'd felt her nose crunch when his fist landed there.

His fingers threaded through his hair and bunched tight.

Shit! Why had she defended the Pratts? She'd even had the nerve to bring up his family history, questioning whether there was any truth to what that bitch Sharon and her horse-faced friend had said. This was all because of them and their gossip, trying to make him and his family look bad.

"Well, it didn't work, did it, Sandy! My family is one of the founders in this town! Such as it is! A one-horse, hole-in-the-wall filled with simple people like the Phelps." He kicked at the broken plate as he strode past. "I need a drink. Where'd that bitch hide the booze?"

He grabbed the handle of the kitchen cabinet over the sink and let it bang against its neighbor. Nothing but glasses. He kept opening cupboard drawers until he saw the bottle of rye whiskey tucked in behind some spices. With a grim smile he yanked it out, spilling small bottles of spice onto the counter below. How long had it been since he'd tied one on?

As he twisted the cap off and poured a healthy glass full of the dark liquid, the memory washed through him. It had been after that night... the one that changed everything. He could still smell the oily grease on the set of concrete stairs in the rink. He snorted. He should be able to smell it—he'd put it there. When the caretaker came upon the broken body splayed on the bottom stair, James Pratt was safe at home with his loving wife.

He belted back almost half of the glass of straight rye, relishing the burn in the back of his throat. Yes, that night had ended Ken Gilpin's career with the Leafs. It's hard to make the team when you're dead. That loud mouth Ken had made James the brunt of one too many jokes. But when he'd cornered James after practice, making sure that the others had left, it had been the final straw. What business of Ken's was it how he treated Sandy? Plus, he'd only tapped her lightly. How was he to know that her eye would turn black and blue?

He took his drink into the living room and flopped down onto the sofa. Even though the rye hit the spot, he'd better ease up or he'd have one hell of a hang-over. Things were bad enough with Sandy storming off. His eyes narrowed. Would she come back? Hell, it wasn't like he beat up on her much. Only once before when she'd nagged him into going to some ice-breaker that the team had organized. There was no way he wanted to know any of them, let alone be friends with them. They were competing against each other, for Gawd's sake. Didn't she know anything?

But it was Ken Gilpin who was the worst of them. He was always cracking jokes and getting the whole team on his side. When James had missed a few passes of the puck, it was hilarious! Yeah right, so funny.

James took another sip of his drink, staring into the dark poison. Who needed Sandy or a spot on that loser team? Not that he was going to make the cut anyway…not after Ken making him look foolish. Sure, he got the job at the insurance company, but it was boring as hell. And with Ken's death, he'd be looking over his shoulder all the time… that was no way to live.

He looked around the room where they'd spent so much time working hard to make it a home. This was not only his escape, it was supposed to be a fresh start for him and Sandy. Instead of peace and freedom, he'd walked into a viper's nest. What was worse was the fact that Sandy had bought into it, hook, line and sinker.

Only once had he ever heard his father talking about Westport. The family had left it years years ago to live in Oshawa. Now that was a shit-hole place, Toronto's so called 'bedroom community' with nothing going for it. His forehead tightened trying to recall what his father had said about Westport. He could vaguely recall his dad talking about the store and the losers who shopped there. Gallagher. Yeah. There was something there about some Gallagher character.

And now that name Gallagher had come up again, with that meddling gossip spreading stories to make him look bad. As if that wasn't bad enough, the moronic Phelps woman was peddling some ridiculous tale about this Gallagher haunting her house! As if. She was just stirring up trouble and that was something he did not need.

He got up to pour another drink and stood looking out the window at the lake. It was grey and cold looking, reflecting the mass of ominous clouds overhead. He thought about getting something to eat but dismissed it just as quickly. He had everything he needed right there in his hand and it was going down pretty smoothly.

Sandy would be back. Where else could she go but back to him? It wasn't like she had many other prospects, not after porking on twenty pounds over the last few years. But when she came back, what would they do? That gossiping Phelps woman would make him a laughingstock if they tried to open up some kind of business. People would come just to laugh at him, not buy anything.

It wasn't right. Why did that family have to move to the village just when he and Sandy had decided to hole up here? At least he had a history with the village, not like the stupid family trying their hand at some half-assed B&B. His jaw twitched, and he marched across the room to sit down at his computer.

If he could find that bitch's website he'd make some changes to it. She was probably too stupid to know how to delete them. He'd fix her website all right. By the time he was finished, she'd be lucky if the board of health didn't pay her a visit. He typed for a few minutes and finally was able to find it. He chuckled as he changed the font to a horror movie style and inserted some pornographic images.

He finished his drink and got up to get another. It was dark out and he couldn't see his yard let alone the water as he stood by the kitchen window. OMG, the internet was such a time vampire, sucking the afternoon away. He'd trashed her website but why stop there?

Why not pay the Phelps' a little visit and ruin those fancy flowers running along their verandah? He huffed. He could probably do some more creative damage if he went in their backyard. They'd never know. They were probably laughing, enjoying having their daughter home, in their own simple world.

He drank the rye whiskey, feeling the warmth in his belly.

Yeah. They'd caused this mess he was in with Sandy, and they'd pay. Ha! They thought their house was haunted, so anything he'd do would be blamed on some hocus pocus bullshit. This could actually be fun. It beat mooning around waiting for his wife to come crawling back.

After grabbing his black leather jacket and a wool cap, his feet practically flew down the stairs. It was surprising how alive and adept he felt after drinking the whiskey. But it helped that he had body mass and was in good shape.

He was hardly aware of walking up the sidewalk when he stood near their back gate, shielded by the shadows. When the light on the second floor beamed, he looked up. Ha. It was the daughter, standing there in her nightshirt with her blond hair falling forward as she lifted the sash. Of all of them, she was the only one that had anything going for her. She was pretty and at least she had enough sense to not live there with those two fools. He watched her pull the blinds, and he cursed. So much for being a peeping tom.

As gently as he could, he lifted the latch in the gate and opening it only a bit, he managed to slip through. He crept slowly up the walkway until he stood on the deck, next to their hot tub. There were lights in two of the rooms, so they were still up, probably with their eyes glued to the idiot box. He looked around, seeing the small pond and waterfall sparkling in the pale light. There were plants and flowers surrounding it he could yank out and throw into the water. The dirt and debris might clog up and then destroy the water pump.

As he crossed the wooden platform, he never noticed the metal watering can set next to the flowers, until he kicked it. The racket of the can banging off his foot and onto the rocks clanged and clattered in the quiet evening. He froze, hunched over, his eyes peering up at the house, specifically at the back door of the sunroom. When nothing happened he reached for the nearest plant and plucked it from the ground. He tossed it into the bubbling water and moved to get another one.

The whole area blazed with light, and he heard the back door squeal open and bang shut. His heart leapt in his throat seeing Peter standing at the top of the stairs next to the door.

"Hey! What do you think you're doing?" Peter kept on descending the stairs, shielding his forehead from the bright light, peering hard at James. "Is that you, Pratt? What the hell are you doing here?"

Finally, James straightened and found his voice. "Just happened to be in the neighborhood, wandering by. Thought I heard a raccoon, but it turns out it's just a weasel and I'm looking at it." Even though he met Peter's stare, he backed up a few steps, going towards the gate. His heart pounded fast in his chest.

The back door opened once more and the bitch stood there, along with her spawn. Sharon came down the stairs after her husband, telling Hannah to stay put. She stood next to her husband, "What do you think you're doing in our yard at night? You don't belong here. Go home before we call the police."

James stood at the edge of the deck by this time. It was only a few feet to the gate where he could escape from them. But he wasn't leaving, not until he got the last word in. "*You* don't belong here! You're trouble makers, nosing around where you don't belong. I thought I'd return the favor and show you what it's like."

Peter put his arm out halting his wife and then he strode closer to James until he was at arm's length away. "Get off my property, Pratt. You've been drinking; I can smell it a mile away. I will count to three and if you're not gone, then we're calling the police." He edged closer, "One…"

"Screw off, bean counter! I ought to pound you into the ground." But his step going towards the gate belied his threat.

"Two…"

Above them, Hannah called out to her father, "I've got 911 on the line, Dad."

"Go to hell! I'm leaving! Just stay away from me and my wife, Phelps! Next time I won't let you off so easy." James ground his teeth as he spun around to walk out the gate, banging it shut behind him.

He heard Peter's footsteps, and then the click as he fastened the latch on the gate.

"Stay away from my house, you washed up nobody!" Peter called from the other side.

Just one last parting shot; he couldn't resist. "You'll never last in this town, you crazy fools! Get out now, while you still can!"

Peter's voice laughed out loud. "You're drunk, Pratt! Go home and sleep it off!"

A murderous rage filled James and he spun around. He could take that stupid gate down with one solid kick!

"I called the police Dad!" Sharon's voice came from the house.

Uh oh. He'd better get moving. The *last* people he needed to talk to was the cops. He walked to the sidewalk. Seeing a car parked on the street, he delivered a mighty kick at the side view mirror, hoping it was Sharon's car. The feel of his shoe crunching it to smithereens was intoxicating.

He snorted. They deserved that and so much more, but right now he needed a drink to calm his nerves. He could practically taste the sharp bite of the alcohol. With every footstep, he felt his blood pressure pound fast in his neck. That skanky old bat and her husband had ruined his life. If not for them, Sandy would be home where she belonged. They could have lived in the village and had a nice life, far from the cesspool that was Toronto. But noooo. Not now.

He yanked the door open and his feet thundered up the stairs to his home. This wasn't over... not by a long shot. And speaking of shots... He raced to the kitchen where he'd left the bottle of whisky. Shit. A third of it was already gone. He huffed. Well, the night was young and still lots of whisky to get him through.

Grabbing the bottle, he stalked off into the living room and plunked himself on the sofa. He barely felt any effects of the liquor he'd consumed. It had to be the adrenaline rush. Well, he'd take care of that soon enough. After taking a few mouthfuls, he held the bottle up, gazing at it.

"Burn them. Burn them allll!"

His eyes lit up. A Molotov cocktail. Yeah. That would get rid of those stupid people and their house. He'd finish this bottle off and recycle it.

Right through the window of that bitch Sharon's daughter's room!

That whole damn Phelps family could join that bastard Ken Gilpin in hell.

THIRTY-THREE

Sharon's eyes flew open staring in fear at the darkness. She lay quietly in bed, the only sound was her heartbeat pounding in her chest. She'd heard something! It had been a thud, like a book falling onto the floor. A quick look at her bedside table showed the book she'd been reading still laying there.

Her heart jumped into overdrive remembering James prowling around in their backyard. She sat up and shook Peter's shoulder. A glance at the clock showed the time as being ten minutes past four. "Peter! Wake up! I heard something!"

He turned to her, blinking the sleep out of his eyes. "What?" But then his mind kicked into gear and he threw the covers back.

Sharon's head turned slightly, cocking her ear to hear beyond Peter's rustling. Had that been glass breaking? It had been muffled like it was coming from outside, but she was sure there'd been a noise. "I think he's back, Peter! I heard something outside, like glass breaking."

Peter's flicked the light on before heading across the room.

"Stay there, Sharon. I'll check it out." He hesitated for a moment and then darted back to get his phone from where it lay charging on his bedside table.

"I'm coming with you! Give me that phone. If it's him, I'm calling the cops." She practically jumped from the warmth of the bed and reached for the phone. "Don't do anything stupid, Peter. He's crazy, and he's been drinking. He might even be armed if it is him! Oh god, I hope, it's just a cat or raccoon."

But after thrusting the phone at her, Peter had left the room, her words not registering. As Sharon raced after him her foot knocked against something lying on the floor. She grabbed for the bookshelf to keep her balance and looked down. There was a book laying there! It was a thick family bible that now lay open. For a moment she froze and a wave of dizziness hit her. Her nostrils filled with the smell of cherry tobacco.

Liam.

She looked around, half expecting to see a shimmering image, so strong was the feeling that he was near. Was this another trick? It had to have been the bible falling to the floor that had awakened her. What the hell? All day it had been quiet, except for the drama with James Pratt and meeting Eve. Now was definitely not the time for Liam to be playing his tricks in the middle of the night.

When she heard Peter's footsteps below, she took a deep breath. "Peter! Wait!" She lurched for the doorway and then held the railing with her hand as she descended the stairs. It felt like she was walking through quicksand with every step. She knew she had to get to Peter fast! She could feel a sense of dread weighing in the pit of her stomach as she walked across the dining room.

When the back door banged, she gasped. Oh my god, was she too late? She had to get out there! What trap awaited her husband? And she knew in her bones it was a trap. Whether it was James Pratt or Liam didn't matter. What mattered was getting to Peter—stopping him!

"Mom!" Hannah's shriek pierced her heart like a knife. But

when the girl's footsteps beat a fast staccato down her set of stairs, her eyes closed for a moment, relieved that her daughter was okay.

She raced to the hallway leading to the family room where Hannah stood in the low light like a specter.

"What's going on? Dad's out there, isn't he? Is it—"

"Stay here!" Sharon sprinted across the sunroom. She prayed she wasn't too late. When she opened the door, about to go down the stairs to join Peter, she came to a screeching halt. Her eyes grew wide watching the scene below.

There were two figures standing at the corner of the house. When the taller one moved closer to the other, catching the light from Hannah's window, she could make out he wore a hat and a faint ember glowed lower in his hand.

There was a shriek before the other figure jerked back. Immediately, a wall of flames engulfed the man's chest, spreading fast down to the ground.

"No! Peter! Oh my god, no!" Sharon's scream became dwarfed by the burning man, who scrambled a few steps away before falling.

Her mouth fell open when a third figure rushed to the blazing mass laying on the grass. "Peter!" She watched her husband lift his T-shirt up and off before using it to bat at the flames devouring the man on the ground.

He paused for a second, long enough to yell, "Sharon! Get some water! Help me!"

Sharon's feet flew down the stairs. For just a nanosecond she felt guilty for the relief in her chest it wasn't Peter on the ground burning. She raced across the deck and grabbed the watering can to fill it in the pond. All the while, the blood-curdling screams of torture sent shivers down her spine.

She was halfway across the deck when Peter grabbed the can out of her hands. "Get another! Hurry! Call 911, Hannah!"

Before she turned to find something… anything to get more water, she saw him. Liam stood next to the house, watching the scene on the lawn. He was as plain as day, standing there in his long overcoat, the cloth hat low over his eyes, the pipe clamped between his lips. He turned to her and nodded before fading into nothing.

She was barely aware that the only sound now was the steam hissing from the blackened form on the ground. There were no screams anymore. Darkness crowded into her vision and her legs gave out. She didn't feel the hard crack when her shoulder connected with the deck.

THIRTY-FOUR

It was two days later that Sharon was once more on the deck below her sunroom. She felt Peter's hand gripping her elbow as he helped her walk across it to the set of stairs. He murmured as he steered her gently. "It would have been easier for you to go in the front door."

On her other side, Hannah held Sharon steady with an arm around her waist. "It's okay, Dad. We've got her. She needed to do this."

Sharon waved Peter and her daughter away and walked tentatively to the chair next to the small pond. She fought a wave of nausea seeing the blackened grass over by the corner of the house. That was where it happened. Where James Pratt had burned to death.

"I tried to cover it up, but the police asked me to leave it alone. I guess it's part of the investigation. What a horrible thing." Peter pulled up a chair next to her and took her hand. "But it's over now, Shar."

"He tried to kill us, Dad! He had a bottle of gasoline that he would have tossed in the basement! It's just dumb luck that he set himself on fire first. And you tried to help him." Hannah slumped onto the deck next to her mother's leg.

Sharon's hand lifted to stroke her daughter's hair. "Not dumb luck, Sweetie. It was Liam who helped us." This was the first time that Sharon said this out loud; although she'd had plenty of time to come to that conclusion. For the two days she'd spent in the hospital, when she wasn't undergoing tests that Peter insisted upon, she'd had time to think—to remember that fateful night.

Hannah looked up at her, "The ghost?"

She nodded. "He woke me up by pushing a heavy book onto the floor, Hannah. I woke your father, and he rushed down to check it out." Turning to Peter, "Did you see him, Peter? He was right there next to James before the fire."

Peter shook his head. "I saw James and then smelt the gasoline. The next thing I saw was James jerk back. He must have spilled gas onto himself, but how did he ignite? The police found the BBQ lighter he must have had with him, a few feet away. Something startled him. I thought it was when I showed up."

Sharon took a deep breath, reliving that night. She could still see Liam standing there, smoking his pipe, watching everything. Her eyes widened. The pipe. Of course. But Liam was a ghost. Nothing about him was real or physical... was it? Then she remembered the touch on her cheek and feeling his breath in her ear as he whispered, *'Ginny'.*

There was no emotion in her voice when she spoke. "Liam was here. I saw him standing next to James and then while James died, he watched. He looked at me and nodded and then he faded from sight." She looked over at Peter, "Was there anything unusual? You know, Liam's pranks—while I was in the hospital?"

Hannah answered, "I stayed here with Dad when we weren't visiting you. Nothing weird happened."

There was a knock at the gate, followed by, "Hello? Mind if we come in?"

Sharon's forehead knotted. The voice didn't sound like Lillian even though she'd said she'd stop by. When the gate opened she was surprised to see Eve Smith's caretaker step inside.

"Mrs. Smith wanted to come over. I told her it probably wasn't a good time, but she insisted." The woman managed a weak smile under questioning eyes.

"It's fine! Come join us."

Peter added to Sharon's comment. "But just for a little while only. Sharon needs her rest."

Sharon squeezed Peter's hand and murmured, "I'm not porcelain. I'm fine, really." She watched the caretaker pop back out and then reappear at Eve's side as she steered her walker through the opening. The old lady's progress was slow but steady as she made her way over to the deck. Peter popped out of his chair and then moved it so that it was across from Sharon.

"Please have a seat. Can I help or get you anything?" Peter walked over, but the old lady waved him off.

"I'm fine. But if you have any iced tea, that would be nice." She pushed the walker, hovering over the contraption like a hunched hawk.

Hannah stood up. "I'll get it, Dad."

But it was Eve who commented, "Thank you, dear. I finally get to meet you." She stepped away from the walker and then sank into the lawn chair that Peter had ready for her.

Sharon smiled at the old lady. "How have you been, Eve? This has caused quite a commotion for you, living across the street from us." She could only imagine with the ambulance showing up, along with the fire truck and police, that it had caused a stir. And for someone in their nineties, it would have been shocking.

"I'm okay. Much better than that Pratt man, thank goodness." She smiled and then shook her head. "Sorry. That's not meant to be funny." She huffed, "Retribution maybe, but still tragic."

Sharon thoughts went to Sandy. The tragedy lived on for James's wife, now a widow. "Yes. Perhaps, but it's still shocking."

Eve slapped her hand on the handle of the chair. "Damned right it was retribution! The Pratts were responsible for Liam Gallagher's death. And I know that Liam had a hand in that boy's death."

That tingly, dizzy feeling swept up over Sharon. "How do you know?"

"I saw Liam that night."

Sharon glanced at Peter, who looked as astonished as she was. "You saw Liam? But Eve, I never told you that Liam was still in this house. He's made his presence known to us, right from the start."

Eve's eyes narrowed, "You didn't have to tell me. I knew it. I've always sensed something about this house, and it wasn't just that I spent many a time here when I was a young girl. I've seen owners come and go but when you moved in, things got... well the feeling I had got stronger. That's why I've been watching your place from my verandah. I normally sit on the water side of my house. It's peaceful back there, watching the gulls swoop and boats go by."

The caregiver, perched on the crossbar of the walker, chimed in. "That's right. Mrs. Smith insisted on sitting on the verandah since you people moved here. And look at all that's happened."

Sharon nodded and then turned once more to Eve. "You said you saw Liam. When? Was it that night?" Could it be that someone other than herself had actually seen Liam? It would be nice to have someone else confirm that she wasn't losing her mind.

Eve nodded. "He woke me up from a dead sleep... although at my age I probably shouldn't use the term..." She smiled at her own joke and then continued. "He was at the end of my bed, as clear as you." Her forehead became even more wrinkled when she added, "I remember the time. It was four, forty-four. Odd, all those fours."

Hannah appeared with a tray of glasses and lemonade, droplets of dew rolling down the sides of the icy, glass jug. After setting the tray on the hot tub cover, she poured a glass and handed it to the old lady. "Mrs. Smith, here you go."

"Thank you, dear. Hannah, is it? That's an old-fashioned name." The old lady took a long sip and then cupped her gnarled fingers around the glass, holding it close on her lap. "Where was I? Yes. Liam. He had that hat, the old-fashioned kind that Irish farmers wear. And his pipe and the long coat. He nodded to me. I can't swear it, but I think he said farewell. Maybe that part was all in my head. But then he left. Faded right before my very eyes."

The caregiver nodded, "She told me about it first thing that morning when I arrived. I swear I smelt tobacco smoke when I made her bed that morning."

Eve nodded sagely. "I deliberately didn't mention the smell of pipe smoke to you. I wanted to see if you noticed it on your own." She looked over to Sharon. "Prince Albert Cherry Vanilla to be exact. I can still see him in my memory filling his pipe from his pouch."

"Cherry pipe tobacco..." Sharon repeated in a whisper.

There was another tap at the gate, and then it creaked, opening wide. Lillian waved and then walked over. "Hi! I hope I'm not interrupting. I wanted to see how you were doing, Sharon."

Sharon let Lillian plant a peck on her cheek before she grabbed the other woman's hand to give it a squeeze. "My partner in crime. I'm fine and you're not interrupting anything. Eve was just telling us about seeing Liam that night when..."

Lillian's eyes were wide as saucers staring at the old lady. "Oh, my goodness. That's amazing. You saw him?"

The old lady's smile was faint when she replied. "I think I saw the last of him. I don't sense him here anymore. That's what I came over to tell you, Sharon. He's gone now."

THIRTY-FIVE

After Eve and her caregiver left, Sharon and her family, along with Lillian, sat in the kitchen drinking tea.

After getting the lowdown on what happened that night, with Sharon seeing Liam, she had more news of the happenings in the village. "Aunt Mary's friend Joan has a grandson who works with the Provincial police. According to Sam, James Pratt was about to be contacted regarding the death of a hockey player—Ken Gilpin. He was a draft pick who fell down a flight of stairs in the arena a while ago."

Peter nodded, "I read about that. They think James had something to do with it."

Hannah snorted, "Would it surprise you if he did? The guy tried to burn our house down with us in it! I never liked that guy. He'd smile at you, but the smile never reached his eyes. His eyes were dead, like a fish at the market."

Lillian nodded before continuing, "I thought so too. But I guess they'll never know if he had something to do with it now."

Sharon snorted, "Another unsolved crime. Kind of like

when Liam was drowned." She peered at Lillian, "Has anyone seen Sandy? I know it's horrible for her, but I wondered if she came back to their house at all."

"No. If she did, no one saw her. She's probably still in shock. According to the obituary, the funeral is tomorrow in Oshawa. Apparently he was raised there and there's a family plot."

"Poor Sandy. She'll probably sell the house. I can't see her ever wanting to come back here to live, not after all that went on with James." Sharon sighed. After a few moments she looked over at Lillian, "Maybe James will haunt that house now."

Peter slapped the table with his hand. "If he's haunting anywhere, it better not be here. You know... after *dying* here. We've had enough of ghosts and hauntings." He looked up and around the room, "No offense Liam if you're still here and listening. Please don't be here, but if you are, no pranks! I can't take anymore of this spooky shit."

Sharon knew that Eve had spoken the truth. Since she'd walked into her yard, she had got none of that weird sense of Liam, not even a niggle. It was strange, but she would miss the old bugger. Well, not such a bugger considering that he'd saved her family. She murmured, more to herself than anyone else, "It's sad and horrible what happened... but Liam had the last laugh after all."

THE *END*

AUTHOR'S NOTE

I hope you enjoyed reading 'The Last Laugh' as much as I enjoyed writing it. It was fun, but also one of the more difficult books that I've written. Why? Because it is based on a true story—about the home where my nephew, his wife and daughter live. It was hard to get beyond personalities to weave an eerie tale that fans of this genre crave.

'Peter' is my sister's kid, a total smartass who pinches his pennies. That's great fodder when it comes to teasing him! 'Sharon' is loveable and cheery although she has a thing about orderliness and you could eat off the floors in their house. Hannah...well what can I say that I didn't say in the novel? She's a beautiful blend of both these fine people and is stunningly gorgeous, a fact that her patients, when she graduates nursing, will enjoy. Spencer is older, a teacher who barely escaped the horrid virus outbreak in China where he works.

When my nephew and his family bought the old home in Westport, they came across the old deed of records and the cryptic note describing 'Liam'. I had to change his name because there may still be relatives alive today. Many of the pranks I laid out in the book have happened and still occur.

Hannah woke to toilet paper being strewn everywhere in her room and bathroom. 'Sharon' actually saw the thermostat being raised when the clicking of the baseboard heaters woke her one night. Many times while vacuuming the electrical cord is yanked from the wall plug, lights go on by themselves and the sound system gets jacked up on its own.

Unlike my characters in the book, they have learned to live with the silly pranks. Sometimes 'Sharon' gets irritated and tells him to knock it off. 'Peter', despite the increased cost of heating when 'Liam' fools with the thermostat gives the poor ghost some leeway—'he's probably still cold from being in that lake.'

Yes, there was a character who was a prankster, gambler

and drinker who was found November 1st, drowned in the lake. Yes, the old newspaper records were destroyed by the new owner. 'Lillian' told me that.

I would like to thank the librarian at Westport, the librarians at Queen's University and the Kingston downtown library, and the historical society in Brockville, for their help in my research.

As always, a special thanks to my husband Jim who not only helps me get unstuck sometimes but also helps with the editing, marketing and cover mock-up we send to our graphic artist, Juan Pedron in Venezuela.

If you enjoyed the book, please take the time to leave a review on Amazon. Writers along with future readers appreciate the feedback.

And, as always, thank you for your readership.

OTHER WORKS

The Hauntings Of Kingston
The Haunting Of Crawley House
The Haunted Inn
The Ghosts Of Centre Stree
The Haunting Of Larkspur Farm
The Ghosts Of Hanson House
The Last Laugh

Paranormal Suspense (The Haunted Ones)
Haunted Hideout
A Grave Conjuring
Haunted By The Succubus
The Haunted Gathering
The Haunted Reckoning
Graveyard Shift

The Mystical Veil
Legacy
Heritage
Forsaken
Ascendant

Celtic Knot
Song For The God
Immortal Wrath
Mortal Enemies